Dawn gritted her teeth. She didn't know why her parents were trying so hard to make Vespertine seem like a great place. They should know by now that there was no way Dawn was ever going to be happy about moving here. No. Way.

Suddenly, she couldn't take it for one more second. She needed a few minutes alone, some time to figure out how to deal.

She rushed to the front door, hoping it wasn't locked. It swung open as soon as she touched the handle — revealing a huge, drooling zombie with green skin and red-veined eyes!

Dawn barely had time to gasp in surprise before the zombie lurched forward and grabbed her.

ROTTEN APPLE BOOKS

Dawn of the Dead

by Catherine Hapka

ROTTEN
APPLE

SCHOLASTIC INC.

ISBN 978-0-545-58840-9

Copyright © 2014 by Catherine Hapka
All rights reserved. Published by Scholastic Inc.
SCHOLASTIC, ROTTEN APPLE, and associated
logos are trademarks and/or registered
trademarks of Scholastic Inc.

12 11 10 9 8 7 6 5 4 3 2 1   14 15 16 17 18 19/0

Printed in the U.S.A.   40
First printing, September 2014

Chapter One

"My life is over," Dawn Romero muttered.

Her father glanced in the rearview mirror. "What was that, kiddo?"

"Nothing." Dawn sighed loudly. "Keep your eyes on the road, okay, Dad?"

Her father chuckled. "Settle down. I've been driving since before you were born."

He winked at Dawn in the mirror. At that moment, the narrow mountain road twisted sharply to the left.

"Look out, Hector!" Dawn's mother exclaimed.

"Oops!" Just in time, Mr. Romero spun the wheel. The SUV skidded around the curve, barely missing a large, crooked tree branch reaching out toward the road. There was a loud crunching sound as the

U-Haul trailer behind the car bounced over the rocky shoulder.

Dawn winced, picturing all her worldly possessions crashing around in the trailer. If her parents had to force her to move away from the only home she'd ever known, why couldn't they at least hire real movers so her stuff could arrive in one piece?

Then she grimaced. Stupid question. She knew *exactly* why they were moving everything themselves.

"Look!" Her mother's excited voice broke into Dawn's thoughts. "There's the town sign. It always looks just the same." She sighed happily.

"I'm not surprised," Dawn mumbled. "It looks like it was carved by cavemen."

She stared at the enormous stone sign and its single word: VESPERTINE. It looked ancient and a little creepy, like a huge tombstone with sickly green moss dribbling across the spiky carved letters. Dawn was relieved when it was out of sight behind them.

But where was the town? There was still no hint of civilization. They hadn't seen a single other car since passing through the bustling town of East Valley almost ten miles back, at the base of the mountain. The forest crowded the road on either side, thick and dark and choked with vines.

There was an unearthly yowl from the back of the SUV. Dawn jumped, and her mother turned with a frown.

"You'd better check on the cat," Mrs. Romero said.

Dawn unhooked her seat belt and leaned over the seat back. Mr. Marmalade was crouched in the corner of his cat carrier. The big orange tabby normally looked placid and friendly. Now? Not so much. His tail was swishing and his ears were laid flat against his head.

"It's okay, buddy." Dawn stuck her fingers through the wire front of the carrier and wiggled them. Usually, that made Mr. Marmalade purr and rub his head against the carrier door. Not this time. He just stared at her, his green eyes wide with terror.

Dawn felt horrible. She wanted to be a veterinarian when she grew up, and she hated seeing any animal fearful or in pain. Especially sweet Mr. Marmalade. Normally, the only thing that upset him was when his dinner was late.

Dawn's mother sighed. "I knew we should have found Mr. Marmalade a new home instead of trying to bring him with us. I'm sure old Mrs. Smith down the street would have taken him in."

"No way. We couldn't leave him behind! He's part

of the family." Dawn turned around just in time to catch her parents exchanging a concerned look.

"This move will be a big adjustment for all of us, Dawn," her father said. "We know it's never easy to start over somewhere new, but if you'll just give Vespertine a chance —"

"Easy for you to say," Dawn snapped. "You're the ones who decided to move. Not me. You didn't even *ask* me."

Her eyes filled with tears, but she did her best to blink them away. She still felt hurt about everything that had happened over the past few months. All her life, her parents had claimed to value her opinions. And Dawn had actually believed them. Why wouldn't she? They always gave her a vote on where they went on their annual family vacation. She was the one who'd picked out Mr. Marmalade at the animal shelter. Stuff like that.

But when it really counted, they hadn't given her any say at all. The decision to move to Vespertine had been finalized, the old house sold, before they'd even clued her in to what was happening. *So* not fair.

Her mother drummed on the armrest with her fingers. "Let's not start this again," she said, sounding annoyed. "We're almost there."

Slumping back against her seat, Dawn played with her charm necklace. Her friends back home had given it to her as a going-away gift. Each of them had given Dawn a different charm, mostly horse-related. There was a tiny saddle, a miniature pair of boots, a cute little riding helmet, and a few others.

Dawn rubbed the biggest charm, a galloping horse, wondering if she'd ever get to ride again. Would they even *have* horses in a place like Vespertine?

"Almost there!" Dawn's mother leaned forward, sounding excited again. "We'll be able to see it as soon as we get to the top of the next hill."

Dawn's dad chuckled. "What, do you think I might get lost? This is the only road into town, remember?"

"I know." Dawn's mother giggled, suddenly sounding more like a little kid than a respected genetic scientist. "Sorry, I guess I'm just excited to be home."

Dawn sat up straight, curious in spite of herself. Over the past few months, she'd heard a lot about the town where her mother had grown up. Now she was about to see it for herself.

The SUV crested the hill, revealing the outskirts of a small town nestled into the mountainside. Dawn was surprised that the houses looked pretty normal.

In fact, what she could see of Vespertine so far didn't look much different from dozens of other towns they'd driven through in the five-hour trip here.

The first house they passed was an old but well-kept Victorian with white siding, blue shutters, and a wraparound porch. A small dog raced down the porch steps and yipped loudly at the approaching car.

"There's a dog here," Dawn said, a little surprised.

"Are you sure it's a dog?" Her father laughed. "It looks more like a walking mop."

The little dog spun in circles, barking more frantically than ever. The front door opened, and an elderly woman hobbled out onto the porch.

"Look, it's old Mrs. Tompkins!" Dawn's mother exclaimed. She waved, but the old woman just peered intently at the car as it passed the house, looking suspicious. "I wonder if we should have stopped to say hi," Dawn's mother added. "I'm not sure she recognized me."

Dawn's father glanced at the clock on the dashboard. "We can go visiting later. Your brother and his family are probably waiting. We were supposed to be here half an hour ago, and —"

SCREEEEEEEEEE!

Dawn jumped as the sudden ear-piercing sound of a siren exploded around them from every direction. "What's that?" she yelled over the noise. "Is there a fire or something?"

Dawn's father winced and shot his wife a meaningful look. "Sounds like you were right," he said. "Mrs. Tompkins must not have recognized us."

Mrs. Romero nodded. "She's always been this town's early warning system."

Dawn opened her mouth to ask what they were talking about. But just then Mr. Marmalade let out a yowl. "It's okay, buddy," Dawn said as she twisted around to check on him.

The screeching siren stopped as suddenly as it had started, leaving Dawn's ears ringing. She glanced out the window. The houses were getting smaller and closer together as they drove on. After a few blocks, the homes were replaced by businesses. All the shops and restaurants had OPEN signs in their windows, but the only people in sight were a young woman pushing a baby stroller and a couple of teenagers on skateboards. All of them stopped and stared as the Romeros' car went by. There was no traffic anywhere, though plenty of cars were parked along the curb.

Where was everybody? It was a beautiful, sunny Friday afternoon. Back home, Dawn knew, the streets of her hometown would be packed with shoppers and kids goofing off after school.

Then she noticed a huge stone building up ahead, looming over the road. Dawn thought it looked like some kind of vampire castle. The place was at least four stories high, with towers at each end and ivy creeping over most of the facade. It seemed almost as old as that stone sign outside of town.

"What's *that* place?" she asked with a shudder. "That's not where you'll be working, is it, Mom?"

"No, Z Corp's lab is out at the edge of town," her mother replied. "This is Vespertine Academy, the school we told you about."

"Oh." Suddenly losing interest, Dawn leaned back against her seat.

Her father looked at her again in the rearview. "Your mother got an excellent education there. Sure you don't want to give it a try?"

"No way," Dawn said quickly. "You said I could go to the public middle school down in East Valley, remember? You promised!"

"Of course," her mother said. "It's just that VA is a lot closer, and, well, your birthday is —"

"You promised!" Dawn said, louder. Her mother could be pushy when she thought she knew best. Dawn should have guessed she might try to talk her into attending her old school. And now that she'd seen the place, Dawn was more certain than ever that she didn't want anything to do with Vespertine Academy.

Mrs. Romero sighed. "All right, never mind. Our deal stands. At least for now."

Dawn bit her lip and stared out the window. Not that there was much to look at out there. They were already leaving the town's small business district behind. Within a couple of blocks, the shops and restaurants gave way to tidy rows of houses.

"Look, Dawn." Her mother pointed to a cute bungalow-style house. "That's where Uncle Charlie and Aunt Kim live."

"And your cousin, Luna, of course," Dawn's father put in. "I'm sure you're looking forward to meeting her, aren't you? It'll be fun for you to have a cousin near your own age to hang out with."

Dawn didn't bother to respond. She'd never met

Cousin Luna. And from what she'd heard, she wasn't sure she *wanted* to meet her.

Halfway down the next block, her father pulled to the curb. "Here we are!" he sang out cheerfully as he cut the motor. "Home sweet home."

They were parked in front of a pretty yellow house with a neatly tended yard. "It looks even better than it did when we bought it," Dawn's mother exclaimed. "Charlie and Kim and my parents must have cleaned up the lawn for us."

"Let's get in there and thank them." Dawn's father unhooked his seat belt. "They said they'd meet us here, and we shouldn't keep them waiting any longer."

Dawn gritted her teeth. How could her parents sound so cheerful when they knew how miserable she was? She didn't know why they were trying so hard to make Vespertine seem like a great place. They should know by now that there was no way Dawn was ever going to be happy about moving here. No. Way.

Suddenly, she couldn't take it for one more second. She needed a few minutes alone, some time to figure out how to deal.

"I've got to go to the bathroom," she lied, shoving the car door open and jumping out.

She rushed to the front door, hoping it wasn't locked. It swung open as soon as she touched the handle — revealing a huge, drooling zombie with green skin and red-veined eyes!

Dawn barely had time to gasp in surprise before the zombie lurched forward and grabbed her.

Chapter Two

Dawn's heart thumped as the overpowering stench of rotting meat surrounded her. The smell was so strong that she couldn't focus on anything else for a second. Then she realized the zombie's super-humanly strong arms were closing more and more tightly around her. She gasped for breath.

"Careful, Uncle Charlie!" she squeaked out. "You're going to suffocate me!"

"Sorry, sorry!" The zombie laughed and released her from his iron grip. "It's just that I'm so glad to see you, Dawnsie — I had to give you a big hug. I can't believe you're really here!"

Dawn pasted a smile on her face. As Uncle Charlie stepped back, she couldn't smell him quite as strongly. But she could see him better. A lot better than ever before, actually. The few times he and Aunt Kim had come to her house over the past few months, they'd been wrapped in layers of clothes, hats, and sunglasses.

But now Dawn got a good look at her zombie uncle. He had auburn hair, just like Dawn's mom. That was pretty much where the family resemblance ended. While Dawn's mother's hair fell around her shoulders in lush waves, Uncle Charlie's sprouted from his lumpy head in isolated tufts. The bald patches on his scalp were mottled and greenish, just like the rest of his skin. A thin line of silvery drool snaked down his chin. His shoulders were uneven, and he moved with an awkward shuffling gait.

Uncle Charlie waved at Dawn's parents, who were climbing out of the car. "Dawn, go right in," he said. "The others are inside. Your gram brought snacks in case you're hungry after the long drive. And your cousin, Luna, is dying to meet you."

"Um . . ." Dawn's stomach recoiled from the thought of food, with the zombie stink floating all around her. "I just remembered, my cat's still in the car. I should get him."

She headed back down the front walk. "Where are you going?" her mother asked as she hurried toward the house.

"To get Mr. Marmalade." Dawn kept moving, ignoring the shouts of glee as her mother greeted Uncle Charlie.

Dawn's dad was fishing around in the back of the SUV. He glanced up as Dawn leaned past him to grab the cat carrier. "How's Mr. M doing?" he asked.

"Not so hot." Dawn winced as Mr. Marmalade hissed loudly. "He's totally freaked out."

Her father peered into the carrier. "Poor guy. We were afraid this might happen. Animals that aren't used to zombies tend to be terrified of them." He shrugged. "I guess they sense the zombies might want to eat them."

"Yeah, I know how they feel," Dawn muttered.

Her father frowned. For a second, Dawn thought she was in for another lecture about how Zombies Are People, Too. She'd heard a lot of those lectures over the past few months. In fact, she'd heard a lot of lectures over the past few months, period. Before that, her parents had never had much reason to lecture her. She had always been a good kid — they said so themselves. She kept her room clean, scooped out Mr. Marmalade's litter box without being nagged, and brought home top grades in all her classes. Especially science. Her mom had always been especially proud of that, telling everyone that Dawn was following in her footsteps.

All that had changed three months ago, along with just about everything else. That was when Dawn's parents told her they were moving to Vespertine — and explained why.

Now her father ran a hand through his wavy black hair, looking distracted. "Why don't you take Mr. M to your new room to let him settle in," he suggested. "It's the first door on the left at the top of the stairs. Then come on down and meet the rest of your relatives."

He hurried toward the house. Dawn followed more slowly. Mr. Marmalade was jumping around so much inside the carrier that she had to hang on to it with both hands. The door was slightly ajar, so she was able to push it open with her foot.

The sound of loud talking and laughter drifted forward from somewhere at the back of the house. But Dawn headed straight for the stairs.

Her new bedroom turned out to be spacious and sunny, with lavender walls, pine floors, and white wicker furniture. If it had been anywhere else but Vespertine, Dawn would have loved it.

She shut the door behind her and set the cat carrier on a pretty floral throw rug near the bed. Then she unlatched the carrier's wire door and swung it open.

"It's okay, Marmie-boy," she said. "You can come out."

Mr. Marmalade remained plastered against the back of the carrier, looking unconvinced. His nose twitched, and he growled softly.

Dawn sat back on the rug and sighed. She'd never seen Mr. Marmalade like this. Normally, he was the most easygoing cat around. He'd even tolerated it when the next-door neighbor's toddler dressed him up in her doll clothes.

"I know you didn't want to move here," Dawn told the cat. "Trust me, I didn't either. Mom and Dad basically gave me no choice. They wouldn't even listen to anything I said. Just insisted we had to move here before my thirteenth birthday next month."

She played with a loose thread in the rug, thinking back to the day her whole life had changed. The day she'd discovered the truth about her family — and herself. . . .

"Dawn!" Her mother's voice floated up from downstairs. "Where are you? Everyone's waiting to welcome you!"

Dawn sighed and heaved herself to her feet. "Wish me luck," she told Mr. Marmalade.

When she got downstairs, her mother was hovering in a doorway. "Come on," she said, grabbing Dawn's hand. "Your family wants to see you."

Dawn reluctantly allowed herself to be dragged into a large, sunny living room. It overlooked the backyard, which sloped down to a thick boundary of tall trees.

But Dawn wasn't focused on the view. The room was full of zombies, and that horrible rotting smell was so strong, she could almost taste it.

"Here she is!" Uncle Charlie grinned and waved from his spot on a leather sofa. "Come on in, Dawnsie. The gang's all here."

"It's so good to have you here, Dawn," Aunt Kim added. She was petite, with striking dark eyes and a big smile. She might have been pretty if not for the blotchy green skin, chunks of missing hair, and thick ropes of drool trailing down the front of her silk blouse. Dawn tried not to flinch as Aunt Kim lurched over and hugged her.

"Come meet your gram and gramps," Dawn's mother said.

"Oh, Dawn." An elderly zombie woman with patches of white hair rose from a chair, leaning on a cane. "It's so lovely to meet you at last."

Dawn caught herself staring at her grandmother's skin, which was even greener than the others'. She tore her gaze away as an elderly man came forward and put a gnarled — but definitely human — hand on Gram's shoulder.

"Welcome to Vespertine, Dawn," he said, beaming. "We're so happy to have you here."

"Who — who are you?" Dawn blurted out.

The old man chuckled. "I'm your gramps," he said. "Your mother's dad."

"You're not a zombie!" Dawn exclaimed, unable to hide her surprise.

"Not an expressed one, no," Gramps agreed with a smile. "Just a carrier, like your parents."

Dawn nodded, too confused to say anything. Her parents had explained how Zombie Syndrome worked: It was a gene, and it turned some people into zombies, like Uncle Charlie and the others, while it left some just as carriers, like her parents. They came from zombie families but looked like ordinary people. But why would a non-expressed zombie — a normal-looking man like Gramps — want to marry a zombie like Gram?

"Luna is so excited to meet you," Uncle Charlie put in. "Where did that girl go, anyway? Luna! Dawn is here!"

"Coming!" a voice called from the next room.

A moment later, another zombie hurried in, holding a tray of drinks. She was about a year older than Dawn, with brown hair that looked mostly normal aside from a couple of patchy spots above her ears. Her skin had a faint greenish tint, and there was only a hint of drool at the corner of her mouth. Dawn couldn't even smell her, though that might have been because the zombie smell in the room was already so overwhelming.

"Hi, Dawn." The zombie girl smiled as she set the tray on a coffee table beside several bowls of snacks, then stepped forward with only a slight lurch to her gait. "I'm Luna. It's amazing to finally meet you."

"H-hi." Dawn knew she was staring, but she couldn't help it. She glanced at Uncle Charlie and Aunt Kim, then back at Luna. "Um, sorry. I was just expecting you to look, you know — worse. More zombie-ish."

"Dawn!" her mother hissed, looking horrified.

"Sorry." Dawn could feel her face getting hot. "It's just I've never seen a zombie kid before, and your parents are so — wait! Does it get worse as you get older?"

"Dawn, that's enough." Her father's voice was stern. "We'll discuss this later."

"No, it's okay, Uncle Hector," Luna said, though she was blushing. "Dawn probably has tons of questions."

"Indeed." Uncle Charlie glanced at Dawn's mother and raised an eyebrow. "Especially since she had no idea about her heritage until recently. You can't blame her for being confused, Angela."

Dawn's mother's mouth set in a tight line. "That doesn't excuse rudeness. Dawn, apologize to your cousin."

"Sorry," Dawn said again. The rotting smell was making her feel light-headed.

"It's okay, really." Aunt Kim patted Dawn on the arm. Her hand felt cold and a little greasy, and Dawn forced herself not to shake it off.

Gramps had taken a seat on the sofa. He gestured to the empty spot beside him. "Come sit down, Dawn. We'll try to answer all your questions."

Dawn was tempted to run out of the room and never come back. But sitting beside her only non-zombiefied relative seemed like a good second choice. She sank down onto the sofa beside Gramps.

"Are you hungry?" Luna waved a hand at the coffee table. "There's plenty of food. Salted and unsalted."

"No, thanks." Dawn was pretty sure she might never eat again. At least not as long as she was stuck here in Vespertine. The Zombie-Stink Diet — guaranteed to work! She almost smiled at the thought. Almost.

Uncle Charlie sipped his drink. "You must have lots of questions, Dawn. How much have your parents told you about Zombie Syndrome?"

Dawn shrugged. "The basics, I guess. I know it's some kind of super-rare genetic thing, and that it runs in families. . . ."

"Like ours." Dawn's mother nodded. "We also explained that most people in the modern world have never heard of it, even though it's been around for hundreds, if not thousands, of years."

Luna leaned forward, gazing at Dawn with sympathetic hazel eyes. "And they told you the rest, right? That even though your parents aren't zombies themselves, they're both carriers."

"Yeah, they told me." Dawn took a deep breath. This was the part she wished she could forget. "They also told me that as the child of a carrier, there's about a twenty percent chance I'll go zombie myself when I turn thirteen."

Chapter Three

"It must have been quite a shock for you to hear that news, Dawn. And finding out about all this so close to your birthday, too," Gram said, tut-tutting softly.

"Enough, Mom." Dawn's mother frowned at Gram. "Trust me, Hector and I feel guilty enough about all this without you guys adding to it."

Dawn's father nodded. "When we met, neither of us had any idea the other was from a zombie family. We didn't figure it out until after Dawn was born."

"It's okay," Dawn told her grandmother. "I mean, it was definitely a shock at first. But I've sort of gotten used to it over the past couple of months." She forced a small smile. "I mean, twenty percent isn't too bad, right?"

She tried to sound confident. But inside, she wasn't so sure. True, she'd almost managed to talk herself into believing it wouldn't happen. That she'd stay normal, just like both her parents. That being from a zombie family was no big deal.

But that was before. Now that she was here in Vespertine, hanging out with actual zombies? It was a little scarier to think about. Especially since her birthday was less than a month away. She definitely didn't want to turn into a zombie — not even a mild one like Luna.

"Don't worry, young one." Gramps patted her on the knee. "Being a zombie isn't what it used to be in the old days, back before the scientists at Z Corp developed the vitamins."

"Vitamins?" Dawn echoed.

"We told you about that, remember?" her mother said. "It's a special serum that helps expressed zombies maintain their human minds and personalities through and after the change."

Dawn didn't respond. If the scientists could do that, why couldn't they do something about the other stuff? The green skin, the patchy hair, the slow, shambling gait, the drool . . .

She didn't realize she was staring at her cousin until Luna smiled ruefully. "I know, it's too bad they can't do anything about the physical effects, right?" Luna picked at the sparse hair over her left ear. "I mean, I don't care that much about the new skin color, and you get used to the drooling. And it's actually kind of nice to be so strong. But I really, really miss popcorn!" She licked her lips, sending a dribble of drool flying. "It used to be my absolute favorite food."

"Zombies can't eat popcorn?" Dawn said, confused.

"That's one of the physical symptoms," Uncle Charlie explained. "We can't taste or digest anything but meat, and we're highly sensitive to salt."

"Oh, right." Dawn vaguely remembered her parents telling her something about that. "So, um, the scientists can't fix that stuff?"

Aunt Kim shook her head. "Not yet, anyway."

"Which is why it's good that Vespertine exists," Gram said. "We have a place to be ourselves."

"So everyone in Vespertine is a zombie?" Dawn glanced at her grandfather. "Or a — a carrier?"

Gramps shrugged. "There are a couple of scientists at the lab and one or two other normals who found their way here and decided to stay. But everyone else is from a zombie family, yes."

Including me, Dawn reminded herself. It was a strange thought. *Really* strange.

"It's best that way," Gram put in. "Outsiders have never treated us well."

Aunt Kim nodded. "These days, they've mostly forgotten we exist, and what memories they have are treated as a joke — just fodder for silly films and such."

Dawn bit her lip, feeling oddly guilty. She'd gone to a zombie movie with her friends back home as recently as last summer. They'd giggled at the moaning, staggering monsters, never suspecting there were real zombies out there. Let alone that Dawn might become one herself. . . .

She quickly shrugged off the thought, wishing she *still* didn't know that part. "So is that why that loud alarm thingy went off when we got here?" she guessed.

"Yes," her mother said. "Mrs. Tompkins sets off the alarm whenever a car passes that she doesn't recognize. That way, all the expressed zombies can get out of sight before any outsiders see them."

Uncle Charlie smiled fondly. "Yeah, that nosy old bag has been keeping an eye on everyone coming into Vespertine for as long as anyone can remember."

"And we're all grateful for it," Gram said. "We don't need outsiders bumbling in unannounced and causing trouble." She clapped her veiny green hands. "But enough chitchat. We should get your things moved in so you can start making this place feel like home."

Fat chance, Dawn thought, wrinkling her nose as the others stood up, releasing another cloud of zombie stink. *There's no way Vespertine is ever going to feel like home to me.*

"Come on, boy." Dawn rested her elbows on the flowered rug, peering into the cat carrier. "Come out. Please?"

Mr. Marmalade stayed where he was, hunched at the back of the carrier. Dawn blew a strand of dark hair out of her face and sat up. She could hear her parents and other relatives talking and laughing as they moved in the bags and boxes from the U-Haul. Dawn had helped at first, but after a while, she'd sneaked away to hide in her room. She couldn't stand the way everyone was acting, as if moving to this crazy place was no big deal. And the smell! How would she ever get used to that? No wonder Mr. Marmalade didn't want to come out. Dawn had learned in science class that cats have a much stronger sense of smell than humans do.

There was a knock on the door. "Dawn?" It was her mother. "Can I come in?"

"I guess so." Dawn got up from the floor and sat on the edge of her bed.

Her mother entered, holding a small shopping bag. "You okay?"

"Not really."

"Oh. Well, maybe this will make you feel a little better." Her mother held out the bag. "It's from Daddy and me."

Dawn took the bag and reached inside, pulling out a bottle of perfume. "Les Cayes?" she said in surprise, immediately recognizing the distinctive label. Dawn had loved the spicy, exotic scent since the first time she'd smelled it at the mall. But it was so expensive that she'd never been able to afford even a tiny bottle of the stuff.

Her mother smiled uncertainly. "I thought it might help you get used to this place."

"Oh. Um, thanks." Dawn couldn't quite manage to sound sincere. Like some perfume was going to make up for having her entire life ruined? She dropped the bottle back in the bag.

Her mother frowned. "Look, Dawn. I know you're not thrilled about being here. I'd hoped you were mature and logical enough to understand why this move was necessary."

"I do understand it." Dawn shrugged. "That doesn't mean I have to *like* it."

"Maybe not. It's your choice whether to be miserable or to try to look on the bright side." Her mother folded her arms across her chest. "Either way, we're not going to let you hide up here and sulk."

"Fine." Dawn tossed the bag on the bed and headed for the door. "I'm going outside to get some fresh air. *If* there's any such thing as fresh air in this stupid smelly town."

She stomped down the stairs and out the front door. Her father and uncle were over by the U-Haul, struggling to lift a heavy box. Not wanting them to notice her, Dawn scooted around the side of the house.

The backyard held a rusty old swing set and the remains of what looked like a vegetable garden. Short hedges of roses and evergreens separated it from the yards on either side. At the back was the thick, shadowy forest Dawn had seen from the house.

Dawn wandered over to one of the swings, tugging on the chains to see if they would support her weight.

"Don't worry, it'll hold you," Luna said, stepping out the back door and shambling down the deck steps. "I tried it out myself the other day." She sat down in the other swing. Now that they were alone, Dawn could tell that Luna did have that distinctive zombie odor. It wasn't as bad as some of the more fully expressed zombies, but it was bad enough.

Trying not to let her cousin tell that the smell bothered her, Dawn stepped away from the swing set toward the back of the yard. "What's on the other side of those trees?" she asked, staring into the tangle of underbrush.

"Nothing. You're right on the edge of town here." Luna kicked against the ground to swing higher. "It's just woods out there for miles."

"Is there a lot of wildlife?" Dawn couldn't help a flicker of interest. Her old house had been smack in the middle of suburbia. The only wild animals she'd ever seen in the yard were squirrels and birds.

"Sure, I guess. You probably won't see much close to town, though."

Dawn nodded, remembering what her parents had told her about animals being afraid of zombies. It was weird to think of a bear or mountain lion being scared of someone like Luna. It also made her wonder how she was going to become a vet if the only animals she ever saw were Mr. Marmalade and Mrs. Tompkins's yappy little dog. She pulled the horse charm out from under her shirt and squeezed it, feeling a pang of sadness.

"What's that?" Luna stopped swinging and peered at the charm necklace.

Dawn stepped back, not wanting her cousin to come any closer. "It's a charm necklace," she said. "My friends back home got it for me."

"Is that a horse charm?" Luna asked.

"Uh-huh." Dawn glanced down at the galloping horse. "I ride. I mean I used to ride. I mean —"

"Seriously?" Luna sounded excited. "My parents didn't tell me you were into horses. So am I — I ride at least twice a week!" She grinned. When Dawn smiled back, Luna added, "It must run in the family, huh?"

"I guess." Dawn's smile faded as she thought about the *other* thing that ran in their family. "But wait, how does that work? My parents told me animals are scared of zombies."

Luna shrugged, kicking against the ground to start swinging again. "Only if they're not used to us. The horses at Vespertine Stables are all acclimated to zombies, though. Ms. Kazemi — that's the owner — is a zombie herself."

Dawn's heart sank. For a second, she'd started to hope that at least one part of her life might still be able to feel normal. Now she wasn't so sure.

Maybe the horses at Vespertine Stables aren't creeped out by having zombies around all the time, she thought, peeking at her cousin's green skin out of the corner of her eye. *But I'm not sure I'll ever get used to it.*

Chapter Four

"You should try the swing," Luna said as she swung higher and higher. Her hair fluttered out behind her, making the bald patches more obvious. "This is fun!"

"No, thanks." Dawn heard the sound of voices from the yard next door. She steeled herself as she looked over, expecting more zombies.

Instead, she saw a pair of normal-looking kids. One was a girl with very pale skin and sleek dark hair cut into a stylish bob. The boy beside her was tall and slim, with a tumble of dark waves falling over his high forehead. Their features were so similar that Dawn knew they had to be brother and sister.

Luna saw them, too. She stopped swinging. "Oh," she said, her voice flat. "Looks like you live next door to the Donovan twins."

"They're twins?" Dawn stared at the pair. "And they're not zombies."

Luna shrugged. "They're still twelve, like you."

Just then, the girl twin spotted Dawn. She nudged her brother, and they both hopped the low evergreen hedge and walked over.

"Hi," the girl said. "You must be the new kid. We heard about you."

"Yeah. Hi, Luna," the boy added. "What are you doing here?"

"Dawn's my cousin." Luna wiped a tendril of drool off her chin and stood up. "Um, we should probably get back inside and help finish unpacking. Coming, Dawn?"

"I'll be in in a sec." Dawn had no idea why Luna was acting so weird and unfriendly all of a sudden. Did she think she was too good to hang out with non-zombies or something?

Luna frowned. "Okay. See you." She hurried off, the rotting smell fading as she let herself back into the house.

The twins barely seemed to notice her departure. "So I'm Jake, and this is Jane," the boy said. "We live over there." He waved toward their house, then grinned. "But you probably figured that out, right?"

Dawn giggled. "Pretty much." She couldn't help noticing that Jake was cute. *Really* cute. When he smiled, dimples appeared in both cheeks, and his eyes sparkled.

Jane was looking Dawn over with her cool green eyes. "So what do you think of Vespertine so far?" she asked, twirling a strand of dark hair around her finger.

"I'm not sure — I just got here. But so far it seems . . . different." Dawn shot a worried look at the twins, afraid they'd be insulted that she didn't sound thrilled to move to their hometown.

But Jane just rolled her eyes. "My condolences on getting stuck here," she said. "Trust me, the second I turn eighteen, I'm out of this place. I want to move to New York City and be an artist or something."

"Really? New York?" Dawn was impressed. "That's cool."

Jane nodded. "I can't wait. For one thing, the shopping around here stinks."

"Yeah, that's not the only thing," Dawn muttered.

"What was that?" Jake asked.

Dawn gulped. If the twins had zombie relatives like everyone else around here, they might be offended if they thought she was insulting the zombies' smell. "Um, nothing," she said quickly. "I mean, I wanted to ask you about something."

"So ask," Jane said, leaning back against the frame of the swing set.

"Yeah." Jake shrugged. "We've lived here all our lives, so we know everything about Vespertine."

"Unfortunately," Jane put in.

Dawn smiled. It was nice to hear someone else be less than rah-rah positive about Vespertine. "Do you guys go to Vespertine Academy?" she asked.

"The zombie school?" Jane snorted. "No way. We talked our dad into letting us go to the public school down in East Valley."

"Me too!" Dawn blurted out. She giggled. "I mean, I didn't talk *your* dad into it, but I told my parents I wanted to go there."

"Awesome!" Jake looked genuinely pleased, which made Dawn's heart flutter. "Maybe we can carpool."

Jane nodded. "Our dad drives us down to school every day. He works from home. I'm sure he'd let you ride with us."

"That would be amazing." Dawn hesitated. "So I guess your dad isn't . . . you know."

"A zombie?" Jake shook his head. "No way. He's, like, three or four generations removed from any zombie characteristics."

"And our mom didn't have any zombie blood at all," Jane put in, sounding proud. "That means we don't really have to worry when we turn thirteen. We only have, like, a two percent chance of changing."

Her twin shot her a warning look. "Are you thirteen yet, Dawn?"

"No." Dawn felt a pang of anxiety, though she tried to hide it. "My birthday's next month. On the seventeenth."

"Really? That's right after ours," Jake said. "We turn thirteen on the seventh."

"Really? Cool." Dawn smiled at him. The last thing she'd expected to find in Vespertine was a cute guy. Especially one as nice as Jake. Most of the good-looking guys back home barely talked to any girl who wasn't a cheerleader or something.

Then again, she supposed Jake couldn't afford to be picky. Most of the girls in town were zombies.

"So what's your percentage?" Jane asked, catching Dawn off guard.

Dawn gulped. Would Jane still want to be Dawn's friend if she knew she had a twenty percent chance of going zombie next month?

"Um, mine's about the same as yours," she said quickly. "My mom and my grandpa are just carriers, and my dad's a non-zombie like your mom." That wasn't true, of course, but it slipped out before Dawn quite realized what she was saying. But no big deal, right? Her dad wasn't from Vespertine, so the twins wouldn't have any way of knowing he came from a zombie family, too.

"Cool." Jane smiled, looking pleased with the response. That made Dawn feel better about the lie. At least a little.

Just then, someone called the twins' names. "That's Dad — gotta go," Jake said. "We'll talk to him about carpooling, okay?"

"Thanks." Dawn watched the twins head home, then glanced at her house. She knew she should go in and help with unpacking. Just then a breeze wandered past, carrying a whiff of zombie smell.

Dawn wrinkled her nose, wishing she'd dabbed on some of her new perfume. Maybe her mom was right about it helping her adjust. At least it would disguise the zombie stink a bit.

In the meantime, she decided she wasn't ready to go back inside just yet. Instead, she wandered to the back of the yard. There was a faint trail leading off between the trees, and Dawn could hear birds twittering in the forest.

She wandered a few steps down the trail and stopped, sucking in a deep, cleansing breath. It was cool and quiet in the shade of the trees. The only smells were plants and moist earth. When Dawn closed her eyes, she could almost imagine she was in the county park back home. She'd spent hours there exploring the trails on foot and on horseback. Of course, the park wasn't nearly as wild and wooded as this forest. She doubted her favorite mount, a round little mare named Magnolia, could even squeeze down this narrow trail.

Thinking about good old Maggie made Dawn feel wistful. But she didn't want to get upset, so she forced her thoughts back to the present. Dawn opened her eyes and walked farther into the woods. The trail was faint, and she wondered what had made it. Did deer or some other woodland creatures come closer to town than Luna thought? Or had the trail been made by people?

After another few steps, Dawn reached a fork in

the trail. She chose a direction at random and kept going. For the next few minutes, she wandered along, trying not to think about anything — just watching for birds in the treetops and for roots lurking to trip her up.

Finally, she stopped to rest, leaning against the scratchy bark of an ancient oak tree. A cool breeze tickled her face, and she realized the temperature had dropped. Glancing up, she saw the dramatic pink rays of the coming sunset peeking through the treetops. Uh-oh. It was getting late.

"Time to go home," she said aloud, grimacing at the thought of calling anywhere in Vespertine "home."

She straightened up and turned back the way she'd come. At least that was what she'd meant to do. The trail had grown too faint to see, and the tree trunks crowding around her in every direction all looked identical. A tingle of panic shimmied down Dawn's spine as she realized she had no idea which way to go.

"No biggie," she muttered, digging her cell phone out of her back pocket. All she had to do was call one of her parents and they'd help her figure out how to get home. Or better yet, come and get her.

But when she checked the phone's screen, there were no bars. Great. Just great. Now what was she supposed to do?

Dawn glanced up again. Already the light was fading, changing the forest from green and comforting to shadowy and spooky. Her heart pounded as she turned in a circle, trying to figure out which way to go. She picked a direction mostly at random, hurrying along in search of the trail. After a few minutes, nothing looked the least bit familiar, so she decided she'd made a mistake and turned back. But now she wasn't even sure she was backtracking correctly! Why did all the trees have to look exactly the same?

"It's okay, it's okay," she chanted under her breath. "Mom or Dad or Luna or someone will notice I'm gone and come looking for me. Soon. I hope. . . ."

She swallowed hard, trying to stop the panic bubbling up inside her. What would she do if nobody came before dark?

She strained her ears, listening for the sounds of nighttime creatures, but she didn't hear a thing. In fact, even the faint birdsong overhead had stopped. The forest was eerily silent.

Dawn gasped as she finally heard a sound — a welcome one. Footsteps!

Whew! She already felt foolish about freaking out. Of course, someone had come to find her.

"I'm over here!" she called. "Dad? Mom?"

She rushed toward the sound of the footsteps. They were coming from just beyond a clump of trees. Dawn wrinkled her nose as a strong smell hit her. Had something died out here?

Then she realized it was just zombie stink. "Uncle Charlie?" she called. "I'm right h — Yipes!" She stopped short as she rounded the trees and found herself face-to-face with a strange zombie.

At least the woman in front of her *smelled* like a zombie. She didn't look much like any of the zombies Dawn had met so far, though. Those zombies had all been wearing normal clothes and acting like regular people, other than the drooling and shambling.

But this woman was straight out of a horror movie. She was dressed in dirty rags; her feet were bare and coated in mud. Green slime dripped from the corners of her mouth. Her black hair was snarled with twigs and leaves.

"Wh-who are you?" Dawn stammered, taking a step back.

"Ouuuuugh!" the zombie woman moaned, staggering toward Dawn. She lifted her hands and lunged forward, her gnarled, greenish fingers grasping and her lips pulled back to reveal hideous, rotten teeth bared toward Dawn's throat.

"AAAAAH!" Dawn screamed at the top of her lungs. She turned and ran for her life.

Chapter Five

Dawn panted for breath as she ran, trying to shut her ears against the moans of the zombie woman. Her shoulders were tense, awaiting the feel of strong fingers grabbing them, and sharp zombie teeth tearing into her flesh.

Suddenly, she realized the moans had faded away. There was no sound of pursuit behind her at all. She slowed slightly. Had she lost the zombie?

Then she remembered: While zombies were stronger than most people, they were much slower and less agile. As long as Dawn kept moving, the zombie woman shouldn't be able to catch up. Unless, of course, there were other zombies waiting to ambush her. . . .

"Aaaah!" Dawn yelped again as a twig snapped nearby. She whirled around, eyes wide.

"Dawn?" a voice called from that direction. A very familiar voice.

"Dad?" Dawn hardly dared believe her ears. "Over here! Dad!"

She raced toward his voice. "Dawn!" her father exclaimed in surprise as she collapsed into his arms. "I heard you screaming. What's wrong? What happened?"

"I — I . . ." Dawn gulped for breath.

"Never mind." Her father's arm tightened around her shoulder. "Let's get you home."

As it turned out, Dawn had ended up less than a hundred yards from the edge of the woods. In fifteen minutes, she was sitting on the couch in her new living room with all her relatives staring at her with concern.

Her mother pressed a glass of water into Dawn's hand, then sank down beside her. "Now, what happened out there?"

"I got lost." Dawn already felt foolish about that part. But she shuddered as she continued. "Then a zombie tried to eat me!"

Her mother gasped. "Dawn!" she exclaimed, sounding horrified. She glanced around at the others. "I'm sorry. I'm sure she didn't mean to be hurtful."

"It's all right, Angela," Gram told her. "Dawn hasn't had a chance to adjust to zombies yet. It's no wonder if she was startled by coming upon someone suddenly."

"No, you don't understand." Dawn clutched her water glass tightly. "This wasn't a regular zombie — you know, like you guys." She gestured vaguely toward Uncle Charlie, Aunt Kim, Gram, and Luna. "This one was really scary. Her clothes were awful, and she made all these horrible sounds. . . ."

Aunt Kim smiled sympathetically. "Don't worry, Dawn. Everyone's afraid of new things."

"That's right, child," Gram said. "It's perfectly normal."

"Yeah." Luna giggled. "Remember how freaked out Dad was the first time he tried sushi?"

That made everyone laugh. Except Dawn. She glared at her parents.

"You guys believe me, don't you?" she demanded. "I'm telling you, this zombie was different. She came after me!"

Dawn's mother still looked disapproving, while her father just seemed uncertain. "I'm sure you thought so, kiddo . . ." he began.

"Different doesn't mean bad," Mrs. Romero broke in. "And I'm disappointed in you, Dawn. I thought you understood that you can't just go around referring to zombies as scary and horrible. It's not polite. Zombies have had enough trouble from outsiders without dealing with cruel name-calling from someone right here in Vespertine."

Dawn gritted her teeth. "Whatever." She yanked out her phone. "By the way, this thing was useless out there. If you're going to force me to live here, the least you could do is upgrade me to a better phone."

Luna giggled again. "Don't bother," she said. "There's no cell phone reception up here, no matter what kind of phone you have."

Uncle Charlie nodded. "Vespertine is just too isolated. It's landlines only up here."

That was the last straw. Dawn had been planning to text all her old friends tonight. Now she couldn't even do that?

"Excuse me," she choked out. Setting down her water glass, she raced up to her new room, slamming the door behind her.

She caught a flash of orange out of the corner of her eye.

"Mr. Marmalade?" Dawn peered under the bed. Green, glowing eyes looked back at her. A moment later, Mr. Marmalade let out a soft "mrowr?" and crept forward to bump his head against her hand. "Sorry I had to drag you to this crazy place, boy," Dawn told the cat, stroking his soft fur. "Trust me, I don't want to be here, either. Even though Mom and Dad keep claiming it's for my own good." She blinked as a thought occurred to her. "You know, my birthday's only a few weeks away. And I only have a twenty percent chance of going zombie, right?"

The cat didn't respond except to let out a raspy purr. Dawn tickled him under his chin.

"Okay, so what happens if — I mean *when* — I don't change?" she said, thinking aloud. "Maybe I can convince them to move back. I mean, they say they only came here for me, right? Dad had to give up his job, and Mom's going to be making less money at the zombie lab. . . ." She smiled, feeling hopeful for the first time since her parents had first spoken the dreaded Z word. With any luck, she might have to put up with living in Vespertine for only a few more weeks!

There was a knock at the door. Mr. Marmalade leaped back, disappearing under the bed again.

"Who is it?" Dawn asked, standing up.

The door opened and her mother peered in. "It's us," she said. "We need to talk to you."

She and Dawn's father came in. Both of them looked very serious.

"If you're coming to lecture me about not being a zombie bigot, I get it, okay?" Dawn said. "But I'm telling you, if you'd seen this particular zombie —"

"It's not about that," her mother said, cutting her off.

Her father bit his lip, looking uncomfortable. "We didn't want to scare you while you're still adjusting to the move," he said. "But now we're thinking we'd better just tell you the truth."

"Oh, great." Dawn rolled her eyes. "The last time you said that, you told me I have a twenty percent chance of going all green and drooly."

Her parents exchanged a look. "Yes, well, about that," her mother said. "See, when I landed the job at Z Corp, one of the other scientists there asked for our family history, for a zombie genealogy project she's working on."

"Right," Dawn's father said. "And you know most of my family is scattered all over Central and South America, right?"

"Uh-huh. So?"

"So I didn't know much about my relatives. But your mother's colleague did the research, and she figured out something we hadn't realized, since we've both been out of the zombie community for so long and, well, we just thought we'd never have to worry about it. . . ."

Dawn's mother looked impatient. "Let's get to the point, Hector," she said. Turning to Dawn, she continued in her matter-of-fact scientist way. "It turns out you don't have a twenty percent chance of expressing your genes when you turn thirteen after all."

"I don't?" For a second, hope flared up in Dawn. Could she be like Jake and Jane? Could her percentage be lower than they'd thought — five percent? Three? Less, even?

If so, maybe she could convince her parents to move back right away! She touched her charm necklace, her heart beating faster. She could go back to her normal life, have her thirteenth birthday party at the stable, just as she'd planned. Her friends wouldn't even need to buy her any gifts, since they'd already given her all those charms. Besides, being home where she belonged would be all the gift Dawn really needed. . . .

She was so busy imagining it that she almost missed what her mother said next. Most of it was gibberish about genetics and percentages and stuff. But her final words broke through.

"So with your family history, Dawn, you actually have closer to a seventy-five percent chance of becoming an expressed zombie."

"What?" Dawn blurted out. "*Seventy-five* percent? You're kidding, right?"

"We wouldn't joke about this," her father said sadly.

Dawn stared at her parents in shock. She'd almost — *almost* — convinced herself that everything was going to work out okay. That she'd turn thirteen and nothing would happen. That her parents would agree to move home, where people smelled normal and the only drool Dawn had to worry about came from the overly friendly Saint Bernard across the street.

But a seventy-five percent chance of going zombie? When the weather report said there was a seventy-five percent chance of rain, Dawn always grabbed an umbrella. Her eyes filled with tears as she felt her hope slip away as quickly as it had come.

"We're so sorry, kiddo," her father said. "If we'd known about this when we got married, we probably never would've had a child."

"Oh, great," Dawn choked out. "That makes me feel a *lot* better."

"You know what he means." Her mother stepped over and put an arm around Dawn's shoulders. "We love you, and we're glad you're here. We couldn't imagine our lives without you."

"Right," her father said, taking one of Dawn's hands and squeezing it. "And we'll love you just as much when you — I mean *if* you do turn out to express your zombie genes. That's why we moved. We think you'll have a better chance of a happy life here in Vespertine with others like you."

Dawn's mother nodded. "Speaking of which, are you sure you wouldn't rather just enroll at Vespertine Academy from the start instead of the public school?" She sounded hopeful. "After all, there's a seventy-five percent chance you'll end up there in a few weeks anyway."

"Yeah, but there's still a twenty-five percent

chance I won't," Dawn countered, swiping the tears from her eyes.

Her parents traded another of their meaningful glances. "Are you sure?" her father asked.

"Positive." Dawn tipped her chin up, setting her jaw. "If I'm going to end up a zombie, I might as well at least try to enjoy my last few weeks of being normal."

Chapter Six

From the moment she woke up on Saturday morning, Dawn *felt* kind of like a zombie. She'd barely slept all night. Every time she'd managed to doze off, she ended up having disturbing dreams. In the worst one, she was blowing out her birthday candles, when she suddenly turned into a horrible, slavering creature like that zombie woman in the woods and then tried to eat her whole family.

Even taking a shower didn't make her feel much better. She dragged herself back to her bedroom and yanked a comb through her thick, wet hair. As she worked on a tangle, she noticed the elegant bottle of Les Cayes sitting on the dresser.

Setting down the comb, she picked up the perfume. If only her friends back home could see it!

They'd be super envious for sure. None of them could afford this stuff. Now that Dawn thought about it, she was amazed that her parents had bought her something so expensive. Normally, her mother thought it was silly to spend a lot of money on things like perfume and makeup.

"Guess they really wanted to bribe me into liking it here," she told Mr. Marmalade, who was watching her from his new hiding place under the desk. She spritzed the perfume on her wrist and sniffed it. Nice. The spicy, exotic scent actually woke her up a little bit. She spritzed the other wrist, and then her neck. Maybe the perfume really would help disguise the zombie smells.

When Dawn got downstairs, her father was in the kitchen, drinking coffee and unpacking a box of silverware. "Morning, kiddo," he said with a smile. "I was just wondering if you were going to sleep the whole day away."

That was the kind of thing he always said on weekend mornings. Of course, back home, Dawn usually slept until at least eleven o'clock. It was barely nine now.

"Where's Mom?" Dawn asked, wandering over to the fridge.

"She went over to the lab. Wanted to get settled in before starting work for real on Monday." Mr. Romero dropped a couple of spoons into a drawer. "She wants to meet the two of us for lunch in town later. You up for it?"

Dawn was tempted to say no. But she knew it wasn't really a question. Her dad might seem a lot more mild-mannered than her mom, but he wasn't going to let her get away with being totally obnoxious.

"Sure, I guess." Dawn grabbed a carton of orange juice.

"Great!" Her dad beamed as if he'd just won the lottery. "This is really a great little town, Dawn. I'm sure you'll learn to love it here."

Dawn focused on pouring the OJ so she wouldn't have to meet his eye. "We'll see," she muttered.

"So where are we meeting Mom?" Dawn asked as she and her father stepped onto Vesper Avenue a few hours later. The town was small enough that it had taken them only ten minutes to walk to the business district. Dawn tried not to look at Vespertine Academy looming at the far end of the next block, instead turning to glance down the street in front of her.

Unlike the day before, the place was bustling. Dozens of people and zombies were wandering — or shambling — around, going in and out of shops or stopping to chat with one another.

Dawn couldn't help noticing that almost everyone they passed, zombies and normal-looking people alike, kept looking at them. Some stared openly, like the little kid hanging on to the hand of a tall zombie woman with almost no hair, and bulging, red-veined eyes. Others were more discreet, shooting glances when they thought Dawn and her dad weren't looking.

Dawn had always wondered what it felt like to be a celebrity. Now she knew. It felt weird.

"Mom wants us to try the Vespertine Diner," her father said, leading the way down the sidewalk. "She says it was the hot happening hangout spot when she was your age."

Dawn just nodded. Usually, she teased her dad when he tried to sound hip. But she wasn't in the mood today.

The Vespertine Diner was crowded when they stepped inside. "I don't see Mom," Dawn said, trying not to notice that at least half the customers were zombies. Probably more than half.

"She wasn't sure what time she'd be finished at the lab," Dawn's father said. "I told her we'd give her a call her when we got here."

"How? Cell phones don't work, remember?" Out of the corner of her eye, Dawn noticed three boys around her age in a booth against the far wall. Two of them were zombies, and all three were staring at her.

Her father chuckled. "Don't worry. We won't have to rely on smoke signals. The landlines here work fine."

A zombie waitress hurried over to them, several menus tucked under her green-mottled arm. "Can I help you?" she said. Then her eyes lit up. "Oh! You must be the Romeros."

"We are." Dawn's father flashed the woman his most charming smile. "Table for three, please. My wife will be joining us shortly."

"Right this way."

Dawn's heart sank when she realized where the waitress was seating them. The booth right next to those three boys.

"Is this the only table?" she blurted out. "Um, I mean, it would be nice to sit by the window. . . ."

"Sorry, hon." The waitress smiled, allowing a thin trail of drool to escape from the corner of her mouth. "Somebody will be by to take your order in a sec."

"Thanks. Is there a public phone here?" Dawn's father asked.

"Sure, follow me." The waitress hurried off, and Dawn's father followed.

Dawn slid into the booth, ignoring the boys. Two of them — one of the zombies and the normal — hung out the end of their booth to stare at her.

"Hey, you," the zombie boy called. He had a broad grin and bright red hair that stuck up in unruly tufts all over his green-mottled head. "You lonely over there by yourself? You could come sit with us."

The other two boys snorted with laughter. Dawn rolled her eyes. "I'll never be *that* lonely," she snapped.

"Ooh, burn!" the normal boy cried, punching his zombie friend on the arm.

The second zombie boy peeked out. "Are you the new girl?" he asked. "The one who didn't know she was a zombie?"

Dawn scowled at him. Did everyone in town know everything about her?

"Mind your own business," she snapped. "And in case you didn't notice, I'm *not* a zombie." She couldn't help shuddering as she said it.

The red-haired zombie smirked. "Not yet," he said. "When's your birthday?"

Dawn didn't answer. She'd just spotted her father heading back across the restaurant. The three boys disappeared into their own booth as Mr. Romero slid into the seat across from Dawn.

"Mom's on her way," he reported. "She said we should go ahead and order for her. So what looks good?"

Dawn glanced at the menu, which she hadn't touched. She cleared her throat. "I'm not really that hungry —" she began.

"Hello, hello!" a jovial voice interrupted. A middle-aged non-zombie man was hurrying toward the table. He had an apron wrapped around his waist and a hairnet over his red hair. "I'm John O'Malley — I own this place. When I heard you were here, I wanted to welcome you personally. Your wife and I are old friends."

"How nice." Mr. Romero shook the man's hand. "Angela always speaks so fondly of her childhood, and I can see why. Vespertine is a charming town."

The sound of muffled laughter came from the next booth. The diner owner shot an irritated look in that direction. "Johnny! What's all the commotion over there?"

The red-haired zombie boy popped into view. "Nothing, Dad," he said. "We were just curious about the new people, that's all."

He smiled innocently at Dawn. She glared back.

Neither Mr. Romero nor the diner owner seemed to notice. Mr. O'Malley flipped open one of the menus. "You'll see that we have a full range of both zombie and non-zombie choices here," he said. "The zombie selections are in the first half of the menu, and the others are in the back."

Dawn flipped quickly past several pages of meat, with the words NO SALT printed at the top of each one. "Do you have any vegetarian dishes?" she asked. At her father's surprised glance, she shrugged. "I was thinking of becoming a vegetarian."

Mr. O'Malley raised an eyebrow, but nodded. "Of course. Last page."

"Good." Dawn scanned the choices. "I'll have the roasted veggie wrap, please."

Her father ordered for himself and Dawn's mother. After Mr. O'Malley hurried off to the kitchen,

Mr. Romero settled into the booth. "This is a nice place, isn't it?"

Dawn shrugged. "It's okay." She was trying not to look at the boys, who were peeking at her again behind her father's back. After a moment, Johnny, the diner owner's son, dashed out of the booth and disappeared. Probably going to get more of his jerky friends to stare at her, Dawn figured.

"Your mother should be here in a few minutes," her father said. "She's really looking forward to showing us around town this afternoon." He cleared his throat. "I hope you'll give this place a chance."

Dawn was still distracted by the boys. "You mean the diner?"

"I mean Vespertine." Her father leaned forward. "We didn't move here to punish you, kiddo. You know that, right?"

Dawn wasn't sure what to say. "I guess," she mumbled, grabbing the saltshaker from the condiment caddy and pretending to find it fascinating. Actually, it *was* kind of weird, given that it had CAUTION: SALT printed on it in big red letters.

Her father sighed and rubbed his forehead. "Okay, we don't have to talk about it right now. But you can come to us anytime with your concerns and feelings, all right?"

Dawn just shrugged as she returned the salt to its place between the pepper and a little stack of artificial sweetener packets. There was a moment of awkward silence.

Finally, her father cleared his throat. "Hey," he said with forced cheeriness. "Your uncle Charlie tells me Luna has a riding lesson every Sunday. Maybe you can tag along with her tomorrow. How's that sound? In fact, Mom and I were talking last night, and we're thinking it might be time to look into leasing you a horse at the new barn. If you find one there you like, of course."

"Really?" Dawn exclaimed. She'd always wanted to lease a horse at her old barn so she could ride more than once a week. But her parents had always said it was too expensive. For a second, she was almost excited.

The zombie waitress appeared with their food. "Who gets the veggie special?" she asked cheerfully.

"Me." Dawn tried not to stare at the bubble of drool on the woman's lips.

Just then, Johnny came back from wherever he'd

gone. Dawn was relieved to see that he was still alone. "Bon appétit," he said, pausing briefly to grin at Dawn and her father before disappearing into his own booth.

The waitress finished passing out their food and hurried off. Dawn poked at her veggie wrap. It didn't look very appetizing, especially compared to her father's juicy burger.

"Um, should we wait for Mom?" she asked, eyeing the tuna melt her dad had ordered for her mother. Maybe Dawn could talk her into trading.

Her father reached for the ketchup. "Might as well eat before it gets cold. She should be here any minute."

Dawn shrugged and picked up her wrap. She hadn't eaten much for breakfast, so she was pretty hungry. Even soggy vegetables would probably taste good enough right now.

She took a big bite and started to chew. Almost immediately, she gagged. All she could taste was salt.

"Gross!" she exclaimed, spitting the bite into her napkin.

Her father looked confused. "Dawn? What's wrong?"

"My sandwich is crazy salty!" She grabbed her

water glass and chugged half of it, desperate to wash the overwhelming saltiness out of her mouth.

Johnny O'Malley and his friends popped into sight over the back of their booth. "Are you making fun of us zombies?" Johnny demanded. "That's rude."

"No!" Dawn took another gulp of water. "I'm serious, it's way too salty. Go ahead and taste it if you don't believe me."

The non-zombie boy jumped out of the booth. "I'll taste it," he offered. He picked up the wrap and took a small bite. "It tastes fine to me," he reported.

The two zombie boys gasped loudly. "You know what this means, don't you?" Johnny told Dawn. "Zombies are super sensitive to salt. If normal food tastes that salty to you, it means you're getting ready to change *right now*!"

Chapter Seven

Dawn let out a shriek of horror. The salt was still burning her tongue. Was she really about to turn into a zombie?

Her heart was pounding, and everyone was staring. It was all too much — she had to get out of there. She jumped up and ran blindly toward the door.

Right outside the diner, she collided with someone. "Dawn?" a familiar voice said. "Where are you going? What's the matter?"

It was her mother. All Dawn could do for a moment was babble incoherently. "Salt," she blurted out, sniffling and wheezing. "Boys said — but it can't — not my birthday yet . . ."

Then her father hurried out, looking worried.

"Dawn? Are you okay? I'm sure this is some kind of mistake."

"What happened, Hector?" Dawn's mother demanded.

Mr. Romero quickly filled her in. "The diner owner's son seems to think this means Dawn is changing early," he finished. "That can't happen, can it?"

"Actually, it's not unprecedented," Dawn's mother began. "There have been rare anomalies in which — but never mind that. I'm quite certain it's not what's happening in this instance." Her expression went grim. "Wait right here." She marched into the diner.

"Dad?" Dawn licked her salty lips with her salty tongue. "What does she mean?"

"I'm not sure. But I have some idea." Her father put an arm around her, staring in through the diner's big plate-glass window. "Let's just wait for her to get back."

A few moments later, Dawn's mother reappeared, her expression stormy. "We'll be having lunch elsewhere," she announced. "But you don't have to worry, Dawn. You're not changing. It was a cruel prank."

"It was those boys, wasn't it?" Dawn guessed. Now that the panic was wearing off, her brain was starting to work again. She felt her face going pink as she realized she'd been punked. "That red-haired zombie kid is the owner's son. And I saw him leave the table after we ordered."

Her mother nodded grimly. "He must have sneaked into the kitchen and oversalted your food. I can't say I'm shocked — his father was a big jokester as a teenager."

Dawn's father squeezed her shoulders gently. "Are you all right, kiddo?" he asked. "Maybe we can try the Chinese place across the street."

"I'm not really hungry anymore." Dawn shrugged off his arm. "Can we just go home?"

Her parents traded a look. "I suppose I've lost my appetite, too," her mother said. "And we can do the town tour some other time. But I actually need to run back to the lab to pick up a few things. Come on, you two can tag along and then I'll give you a ride home."

Dawn opened her mouth to say that she'd rather just walk. Then she looked at all the zombies shambling around town. Maybe she didn't feel like walking home after all.

Soon, they were in the car driving slowly down Vesper Avenue. Dawn slumped in the backseat, staring out the window. How was she ever going to survive living here for even a few weeks? Or possibly longer, if . . .

No. She refused to think about that.

The forbidding stone facade of Vespertine Academy came into view. Dawn shuddered when she saw it. Those nasty boys from the diner probably went there, which was just another reason it would be horrible if she was forced to go there. She turned and looked out the opposite window until they were well past the building.

Unlike the zombie school, the zombie lab looked surprisingly normal — a lot like her mother's old workplace, actually. It was located a mile or so beyond the edge of town and consisted of a large glass-and-steel building with a well-groomed lawn surrounding it.

"Come on in," Dawn's mother said as she cut the engine. "A few of my colleagues are in today. I'm sure they'd love to meet you."

"I think I'll wait in the car," Dawn said.

Her father turned and frowned. "Come on, kiddo," he said. "Your mom wants to show off her work.

Don't let those boys totally ruin our day, all right? It'll only take a minute."

Dawn was about to argue. Then she noticed a gardener weeding a flower bed at the edge of the parking lot just a few yards from their car. He was a zombie, with wispy patches of grayish hair and a big, mottled green nose.

"Okay," she muttered. "I guess I'll come in."

The lab looked normal inside, too. Well, mostly. In the lobby was a life-size bronze statue of an old-man zombie, complete with a trickle of drool at the corner of his mouth and a gnarled hand clutching an old-fashioned pocket watch.

Dawn's mother saw her staring at the statue. "That's the founder of Z Corp," she said. "He's the one who made the first big breakthrough that led to the development of the serum."

"What if someone who's not from Vespertine came in here and saw that thing?" Dawn stared at the bronze zombie. "It's kind of a giveaway, isn't it? I mean, a statue can't exactly hide whenever Mrs. Tompkins's alarm goes off."

Her mother smiled. "Very logical point, Dawn," she said, sounding proud. "Actually, I'm told that statue is on rollers so they can push it out of sight on the rare occasions the lab has a planned non-zombie visitor. Of course, when the alarm goes off unexpectedly, I'm sure they just lock the doors so no one can wander in."

"Hmm." Dawn stared at the bronze zombie as they passed.

Much like the lobby, the actual labs looked mostly normal, too. But in addition to the periodic table of the elements and other normal scientific stuff, there were diagrams on the walls showing the various stages, symptoms, and degrees of Zombie Syndrome.

Dawn was surprised to see several people hard at work at computers or lab tables. One of them, a man about her grandfather's age, looked up from his keyboard. He wasn't a zombie, though his skin was mottled with age spots. He had intelligent brown eyes and wire-rimmed glasses perched atop his half-bald head.

"Angela! You're back," the old man exclaimed, rushing over. "Is this your family?"

"Yes. This is my husband, Hector, and our daughter, Dawn."

"Ah, Dawn. I've heard all about you." The old man peered at her curiously. "Welcome to Z Corp. I'm Dr. Pruitt."

"My new boss," Dawn's mother told her with a smile. "And the most brilliant scientist of his generation."

"Don't say that," someone called out with a laugh. "It'll go to his head!"

Dawn looked over to see who had spoken. A zombie woman had just risen from her lab table and was shambling toward them. She had thick dark hair and big hoop earrings. Her lab coat hung open in the front to reveal a T-shirt with the words ZOMBIES RULE, NORMALS DROOL! spelled out in pink rhinestones.

"This is Dr. Torres, another brilliant scientist," Dr. Pruitt said.

"Call me Dr. Nancy." She grinned at Dawn. "Do you like my T-shirt?"

Dawn realized she'd been staring. "Um, sorry," she blurted out. "I — I never saw one like that before."

"It's just a joke," Dr. Pruitt said with a chuckle. "She had it made after she caught me napping at my desk one day."

"With enough drool for three zombies all over the notes he was supposed to be reading." Dr. Nancy laughed loudly, sending her own drool flying.

Dawn smiled politely, though she didn't think the joke was that funny. "So you're all here working even though it's Saturday?" she said. "Don't you get the weekend off?"

"Of course," her mother said. "But the scientists and other staff here are very dedicated."

Dr. Pruitt nodded. "We know the advances made right here at Z Corp have already made life much easier for generations of zombies, and we want to do even more."

"That's right," Dr. Nancy agreed. "Maybe someday we won't have to hide away here in Vespertine anymore. Maybe we'll reach a point where Zombie Syndrome won't seem any stranger to the outside world than diabetes or asthma."

Dawn's father smiled. "I think it's great. Don't you, kiddo?" He nudged Dawn.

"Sure, I guess." Dawn was thinking about what the scientists had said. "Does that mean you're working on a real cure? Like, to stop people from turning into zombies at all?"

Dr. Pruitt chuckled. "Not yet. I doubt we'll ever eradicate ZS completely. But we're always improving zombies' standard of living."

Dawn's heart sank. So there was no way out. If she went zombie next month, that was it. She would be stuck here in Vespertine — forever.

Chapter Eight

On Sunday afternoon, Dawn sat on the front steps of her house. The door was standing open, and Mr. Marmalade was crouched in the hallway at the bottom of the stairs. It was the farthest he'd ventured from Dawn's bedroom since they'd moved in.

"It's okay, boy," Dawn called. "You can come out and look around if you want."

Mr. Marmalade's tail swished. He took another slow, cautious step forward and sniffed the air.

Suddenly, his ears went flat. With a loud growl, he turned and dashed back upstairs.

"Marmie-boy?" Dawn called. Glancing toward the street, she saw Luna stopping her bike on the sidewalk in front of the house. Obviously, the cat had caught a whiff of zombie scent and panicked.

Maybe I should put some of my new perfume on him, Dawn thought, taking a quick sniff of her own wrist. *It's definitely helping me. I don't notice the crazy smells quite as much.*

She sniffled and cleared her throat. Her head felt a little stuffed up today. Maybe she was coming down with a mild cold, and that was why the zombie smells didn't seem as bad.

"Ready to go?" Luna asked, hurrying up the front walk.

"Sure. Thanks for letting me tag along." Dawn stood up. She was wearing her favorite breeches and her well-worn paddock boots. Her riding helmet was on the step beside her.

Just then, Jake and Jane emerged from their house. Jane was wearing a tunic top sort of like one Dawn had seen in a fashion magazine recently. Jake was just wearing jeans and a sweatshirt, but he looked cuter than ever. The twins spotted Dawn and Luna and came over.

"What's up, Dawn?" Jane said, ignoring Luna. "We were wondering where you were yesterday." She smirked. "I thought maybe Vespertine had driven you crazy already and you ran away back to civilization."

"Not quite." Dawn was flattered to think that the twins had been looking for her. She sneaked a peek at Jake. He was smiling at Luna.

"Off to the stables, Luna?" he asked.

"Yeah," Dawn said before Luna could respond. "Um, you guys could come along if you want." She glanced at her cousin. "That would be okay, right?"

"Sorry, we can't." Jane didn't sound that sorry at all. "Our dad's taking us shopping out in the normal world. He says we can pick out whatever we want for our birthday even though it's a little early."

"Really? That sounds like fun." Dawn held her breath, wondering if they'd invite her along. She'd been looking forward to riding, but the stable would be there another day.

But Jane just said, "Yeah," then started digging around in her purse.

"Hey, speaking of our dad," Jake told Dawn, "he said you can definitely ride with us to school. Just have your parents call him to set it up."

"Really? Cool." That made Dawn feel better. Even though East Valley was only about ten miles away, it took a long time to get there on the twisty mountain road. She would probably get to spend almost an hour a day in the car with the twins.

"Come on, Dawn," Luna spoke up. "We should go or we'll be late for my lesson."

She hurried off toward her bike without waiting for a response. Dawn shrugged at the twins. "I guess I'll see you in the morning."

Soon, she and Luna were biking across town. "Listen, Dawn," Luna began. "I wasn't going to say anything, but I feel like I should warn you about the Donovan twins."

"What about them?" Dawn dodged a stone on the sidewalk.

"They're snobs, that's what. They're always bragging about their low percentage, like they think it makes them better than everyone else in Vespertine." Luna frowned. "It's not right. Zombies are people, too!"

Dawn almost rolled her eyes. That sounded like something her parents would say.

"I don't think they're snobs," she said. "I like them. Besides, I'll be living next door and going to school with them. So I might as well try to get along with them, right?"

Luna bit her lip. "I still don't get why you aren't going to Vespertine Academy," she said. "It's a great school."

Dawn just shrugged. She didn't feel like explaining it to her cousin. Besides, Luna probably wouldn't understand how Dawn felt. She was a zombie — she didn't have much choice about where to go to school.

"So how far is it to the stable?" Dawn asked instead.

"Not much farther." Luna took the hint and let the subject of Jake and Jane drop. She and Dawn talked about horses for the rest of the bike ride.

As soon they rode up the driveway of Vespertine Stables, Dawn took a deep breath and smiled. "I've missed the smell of horses." She tried to ignore the zombie smells mixing in with the pleasant horsey scent.

The stable was smaller and more rustic than Dawn's old lesson barn. The barn was painted dark red, and there were several paddocks, a riding ring, and a couple of pastures off to one side. On the other side were the woods.

"Come on," Luna said, dropping her bike near the entrance. "Let's go find Ms. Kazemi. I told her you were coming."

The stable owner was a tall, slim zombie with dark hair and only a slight lurch. She smiled and looked Dawn up and down, taking in her riding gear.

"Looks like you've done this before," she said. "Why don't you saddle up Skip and I'll see what you can do."

Luna showed Dawn the right stall. Skip was a stout chestnut gelding with a crooked blaze and a sweet expression. Dawn tacked him up quickly and led him to the ring, where Ms. Kazemi was waiting.

It felt good to be back in the saddle. The first couple of times around the ring, Skip kept trying to slow down or stop near the gate. But Dawn made him keep going, and after that, he walked, trotted, and cantered obediently. Ms. Kazemi gave Dawn tips once in a while. She reminded Dawn a little of her riding instructor back home. Well, except when Dawn looked at her and remembered that she was a zombie. Luckily, Skip didn't seem to care about that. Neither did the big brown dog that wandered out halfway through the lesson and sat down at Ms. Kazemi's feet. Maybe that meant there was hope for Mr. Marmalade.

"Very good." Ms. Kazemi seemed pleased when Dawn pulled up. "You ride well, Dawn. You're welcome to join your cousin's intermediate group lesson today if you like."

Luna emerged from the barn just in time to hear her. She was leading a cute little bay mare. "That's awesome, Dawn!" she said. "Our lessons are super fun."

Dawn was about to agree to join the lesson. But then two other girls led their horses out of the barn. Both were zombies. One had only a few tufts of curly black hair left on her head. The other girl's skin was so green she looked like she was covered in mold.

"Um, I'm not sure I'm ready for a lesson today," Dawn told Ms. Kazemi. "Would it be all right if I went on a trail ride instead?"

"By yourself?" The stable owner looked dubious. "I don't know."

Luna smiled. "I could go with her," she offered.

"No, that's okay," Dawn said quickly. "Uh, I don't want you to miss your lesson. Besides, I kind of want to be alone for a little while."

"Oh." Luna's smile faded. "Um, okay."

"I used to trail ride all the time at my old barn," Dawn told Ms. Kazemi. "And I'll be careful. I swear."

The stable owner studied her. "Well, I suppose it would be all right," she said at last. "Skip is our best trail horse — he'll take care of you. Just be sure to stick to the blue trail, okay? It's clearly marked. That's the only trail students are allowed to ride on by themselves. And don't stay out for more than forty minutes or so."

"Okay." Dawn picked up the reins. "Come on, Skip. Let's go."

The blue trail began right behind the barn. It was wide and smooth, marked by blue triangles painted on the tree trunks. Skip seemed happy to be out there; this time, Dawn didn't have to force him to keep moving. Soon, the stable was out of sight behind them.

Dawn let out a deep breath and smiled. Skip was a great horse, and riding made her feel happier than she'd felt since arriving in Vespertine. Everything else in her life might have changed, but at least she still had this.

After a few minutes, they reached a fork in the trail. Dawn brought Skip to a halt. He lowered his head, nibbling at a stray bit of grass near the trail.

"Looks like the blue trail loops around to the right," Dawn said aloud.

She started to turn the horse that way. Then she hesitated, glancing down the other trail. It looked a lot more interesting. Besides, she didn't want to get back to the stable too soon.

"What do you think, Skip?" she said. "Want to do a little exploring?"

She'd let the reins go slack. Skip took a step toward the unmarked trail, grabbing another bite of grass. Dawn grinned.

"Okay, if you say so," she said. "Let's go!"

She turned the horse to the left. Skip pricked his ears forward as if he were just as eager to explore as she was.

Dawn felt a pang of uncertainty, but she shook off the feeling. She had Skip, and horses always knew their way home — if they got lost, she could just give Skip his head and he'd take them back to the stable. No big deal.

So they rode farther into the woods, which were quiet and pleasant. Skip ambled along, occasionally slowing to pick his way down a hill or over a rocky part of the trail. A couple of times, Dawn had to duck to avoid low-hanging branches, and once, a thorny vine left a scratch on her arm.

She didn't mind, though. Riding out here was a lot more interesting than it was in the boring suburban park back home. Being in these woods made her feel like a real explorer. She had a feeling she could ride out every day and never see all there was to see.

Skip let out a sudden snort as something rustled in the brush beside the trail. "What is it, boy?" Dawn asked, giving him a pat. "Probably a rabbit or maybe a —"

She cut herself off with a gasp. The wild zombie woman was right in front of them!

Chapter Nine

"Whoa!" Dawn cried as Skip took a quick few steps backward, almost stumbling over a root.

The zombie woman gurgled and lurched forward, gesturing wildly. She looked worse than ever. Her hair looked like a rat's nest, and her face was streaked with dirt and drool.

"Who are you?" Dawn cried. "What do you want?"

The zombie woman only grunted in response. Then she leaped forward, flinging a handful of leaves at the horse.

That was all Skip could take. Spinning around, he gathered his haunches and launched himself down the trail at a gallop.

"Whoa! Skip, stop!" Dawn yelled, her heart racing. She'd lost control of the reins when the horse bolted, and one of her feet had come out of the stir-rup. It was all she could do to cling on for dear life.

She barely stayed in the saddle as Skip raced toward home. He slowed down a little as he skidded around the turn onto the blue trail, and Dawn managed to jam her foot back into the stirrup and gather up the reins. A few yards from the stable, she was finally able to bring Skip back to a brisk trot, and then a walk.

Dawn caught her breath and looked around. Luckily, nobody saw them returning. She could hear the lesson still going on, but the riding ring was out of view around the corner of the barn. Dawn was relieved — she didn't want to get in trouble on her first day at the new stable.

Sliding down from the saddle, Dawn realized her whole body was trembling. "You saw her too, right, Skip?" she whispered, stroking the horse's sweaty neck. "Too bad you can't talk. Maybe then somebody might believe me."

Dawn wanted to tell Ms. Kazemi about the scary zombie woman. But why bother? Her own parents hadn't believed her last time. Besides, she didn't want the stable owner to find out she'd left the marked trail.

By the time Dawn finished untacking Skip and walking him around to cool him off, the lesson still hadn't finished. Usually, Dawn loved hanging around stables even when she wasn't riding, but today she just wanted to get home. She left a note for Luna and took off on her bike.

"Hi," Dawn said as she slid into the backseat of the Donovans' car the next morning. "Thanks for letting me ride with you."

"You're welcome, Dawn." Mr. Donovan was a pale man with a quiet voice and sad gray eyes. "The twins have told me so much about you."

Dawn just smiled politely. How could they have told him anything? They barely knew her.

Jake was in the front seat. "Morning, Dawn," he said in his usual friendly way.

"Morning," Dawn said. She was nervous about starting a new school, even though she'd assured her dad that she didn't need him to take her in on the first day. But seeing the twins made her feel a little better. At least she already had some friends at Vesper County Junior High.

Jane leaned closer and sniffed as Dawn put on her seat belt.

"Is that Les Cayes?" she asked, sounding impressed.

"Yeah." Dawn said, pleased. She had dabbed on a generous amount of her perfume that morning. She couldn't help worrying that the zombie smells from Vespertine might stick to her clothes or hair. "My parents got it for me."

"Lucky!" Jane said. "I tried to get Dad to buy me some for my birthday, but they didn't have it at the lame little mall in East Valley."

"Too bad," Dawn said. "You can use some of mine if you want."

"Really?" Jane's eyes lit up. "Awesome! That's really nice of you, Dawn."

Dawn returned her smile. Then she glanced out the window. The twins' father had taken a shortcut, and they were already driving past Mrs. Tompkins's house on the way out of town.

Soon, they were on the winding road down the mountain. Dawn felt herself relax more and more the farther they got from Vespertine. Maybe the next few weeks wouldn't be so terrible after all. She would get to spend every school day with the twins in East

Valley. In between, she could hang out at the barn and try to ignore the zombie smells. Before she knew it, her birthday would be here and she could start working on her parents to move back home.

Either that, or her birthday would come and her life as she knew it would be over. But she wouldn't think about that possibility.

East Valley was a little bigger than Vespertine, with several fast-food restaurants, a mall, and even a bowling alley. The school was a squat brick building atop a hill. As they pulled up, tons of kids were hanging out in the parking lot and on the front walk. It all looked so normal that Dawn almost cried.

But she got ahold of herself just in time. "Ready?" Jane said.

Dawn thanked Mr. Donovan for the ride, then climbed out of the car and followed the twins toward the door. Jane had her backpack slung over one shoulder. With her other hand, she was fiddling with a silver charm hanging on a thin chain around her neck.

"Cool necklace." Dawn leaned closer for a better look. The charm was a unique-looking squiggle with a little star in the middle. "I've never seen one like that."

"It was my mom's," Jane said. "It used to be one-half of her favorite pair of earrings. Dad says I used to play with them when I was a baby." Her eyes went all distant for a second. "It's the only thing I have of hers. The other earring was buried with her."

"Oh." Dawn felt a little awkward. She'd figured out that the twins' mother wasn't around, but she hadn't realized that it was because she'd died. For some reason, Dawn had assumed she'd gotten fed up with the zombie lifestyle and left. Maybe because that was exactly what Jane claimed she wanted to do when she grew up. "Um, how did she die?" Dawn blurted out.

Jane's expression darkened. "I don't want to talk about it," she snapped. Spinning on her heel, she marched into the school without a backward glance.

"Sorry about that." Jake came up beside Dawn. "She's a little sensitive about our mom." He shrugged. "Mostly because Dad won't tell us exactly how she died. Just that it was some kind of disease. Like it's not bad enough we have to worry about you-know-what." Shooting a glance toward the mountain looming in the distance, he rolled his eyes. "We also have to wonder if we're going to come down with cancer or something, too."

He didn't sound very worried, though. Dawn wondered if he ever worried much about anything. He didn't seem to. That was one of the things she liked about him. Being around him almost made her forget to worry about stuff, too.

"Come on," he said. "You probably need to stop in at the office to pick up your schedule. I'll show you where it is."

By the end of fourth period, Dawn was already feeling at home at VCJH. It was nice to be back in the normal world again. She walked out of English class with Jake and Jane.

"Time for my favorite class of the day," Jake said. "Lunch!"

Soon, Dawn was following the twins through the crowded cafeteria to their usual table. Three kids were already seated there. Jane pointed to each of them in turn. "That's Xander," she said. "And Yasmin, and Zack."

"X-Y-Z," Dawn said. "Cool."

Zack grinned at her. He was tall and gangly with spiky blond hair and big ears. "Uh-oh, you might be too smart to sit with us," he said. "Or at least with Yas."

Yasmin, a pretty dark-haired girl, punched him in the arm. "So, Dawn, where are you from?" she asked. "You don't live in the same weirdo town as the twins, do you?"

"She does! Lucky her." Jake glanced up from unwrapping his sandwich and grinned. "She's stuck with us weirdos."

Dawn smiled uncertainly. What were they talking about? She thought the outside world didn't know anything about the zombies in Vespertine.

Jane shot Dawn a warning look. "Dawn hasn't lived there long," she told the others breezily. "She probably hasn't even heard all the rumors about Z Corp yet."

"Yeah." Xander stared at Dawn. He had a short Afro and glasses. "Hey, Dawn, it sounds like you've got the sniffles. I hope you're not already poisoned by living up there."

"What do you mean?" Until that moment, Dawn hadn't really even noticed that her nose was running. She coughed, then grabbed a napkin and blew her nose. Obviously, that mild cold she'd noticed yesterday was still hanging around.

Jake laughed. "That's one of the rumors. People

think Z Corp dumps dangerous chemicals in the woods outside Vespertine."

"What?" Dawn exclaimed, thinking about the clean, well-run lab where her mother worked. "Um, what do you mean?"

"Scary, right?" Yasmin's eyes widened. "My older sister is really into the environment and stuff, and she thinks they've totally poisoned the air and water up there. She says it's only a matter of time before people start coming down with weird diseases and stuff."

Zack snorted. "Your sister's nuts." He shot a side-long look at Dawn. "Still, you've gotta wonder. Hey, Dawn, can you feel yourself growing tentacles or anything?" He wiggled his fingers at her.

"Or seen any three-headed monsters running around the woods?" Xander added with a grin.

"Um, not yet." Dawn tried to sound normal. But the mention of monsters in the woods made her flash back to that weird zombie woman.

It also made her want to tell these kids that those silly rumors weren't true. Z Corp was all about help-ing people — well, helping *zombies*, actually — not hurting them. She sneaked a look at the twins.

Neither of them seemed bothered by what the other kids were saying. Jane was sipping her chocolate milk calmly, and Jake was laughing along with the other guys.

Okay, if it didn't bother them, she was going to try not to let it bother her. Still, she was starting to wonder if going to school here was going to be quite as normal as she'd hoped.

Chapter Ten

For the rest of the week, Dawn stayed pretty busy. She did her best to catch up in all her new classes, which luckily wasn't too hard. Her science class was at least a full month behind the advanced science lab at her old school, and most of her other classes were about the same as her old ones.

Things were improving a little at home. Mr. Marmalade gradually stopped hiding under the furniture every time a zombie came to the door. He even stayed in view at the top of the stairs, watching suspiciously, when Dawn's grandparents came to dinner on Thursday night.

Dawn could tell that her parents were pleased that she seemed to be adjusting so well. "I'm glad you talked us into letting you go to the public school," her dad said, sipping his coffee and watching her stuff her books into her backpack on Friday morning. "It seems to suit you."

"Yeah, it's okay." Dawn didn't bother to tell him that she was just biding her time. Waiting for her birthday. Hoping she could go back to her normal life.

"Have a great day, kiddo," her dad said as she headed for the door.

"Thanks." Dawn hurried over to the Donovans' house. She got there just as Jake and Jane emerged.

"Hi," Jane greeted her. "Did you finish the science homework?"

"Yeah. Want to check our answers on the ride?" Dawn offered.

Jake rushed toward the car. "Shotgun!" he called with a laugh.

"Hey, it's my turn to ride in front today," Jane protested.

Dawn smiled as she watched the two of them fight over the front seat. But she also felt a weird little twinge of sadness. She was really starting to like both the twins. Jane seemed sarcastic at first, but underneath that slightly prickly exterior, she was actually smart, funny, and generous. As for Jake,

Dawn had liked him from the start, and she only liked him more, the better she got to know him. Even after only a week, it bothered her to think about leaving the twins behind when she moved back home. Maybe they could come visit her there sometime.

Dawn cleared her throat, then coughed. That reminded her of another thing that had been bothering her more and more all week. Ever since that first day at lunch, she couldn't help noticing that she seemed to have an almost constant need to clear her throat, plus excess saliva and an annoying little cough.

At first she'd told herself it was a cold. Then allergies. But she was starting to wonder — what if it wasn't either of those things? What if her symptoms were early signs of the change, the first stages of zombie drool? After all, her birthday was only a couple of weeks away now. . . .

"Coming, Dawn?" Jake called from his spot in the backseat.

Dawn sucked in some extra saliva, then smiled. "Coming."

*   *   *

Sunday afternoon was exactly two weeks before Dawn's birthday. She put it out of her mind as she ran a brush over Skip's chestnut coat. She'd gone back to the stable with Luna, promising to join the group lesson this time. Dawn still wasn't sure she'd be able to concentrate on her riding with all those zombies around. But somehow, trail riding didn't seem quite as fun now that Dawn knew the scary zombie woman was still out there in the woods.

"Quit that, Rosie!" Luna's voice drifted over from the next stall. She sounded frustrated.

Dawn poked her head over the door of Luna's stall. "Everything okay?"

Luna waved the metal hoof pick she was holding. "She keeps pulling her foot away when I try to pick it out!"

"You're in luck," Dawn said with a smile. "I happen to be an expert with a hoof pick. The pony I first learned to ride on knew every trick in the book."

Luna giggled. "Okay, prove it," she said, holding out the hoof pick.

Dawn entered the stall and took the pick. "Be a good girl," she warned the horse, the same pretty bay mare Luna had ridden the week before.

Then she gently but firmly took hold of the mare's left front hoof, lifting it into the best position for cleaning. The mare held it there for only a second or two before leaning away and trying to slam it back down.

"Ah-ah-ah!" Dawn said, hanging on to the hoof with both hands. "Naughty girl."

The mare looked surprised. She tried once more to pull her foot away, but once again Dawn was ready for her.

"Wow!" Luna sounded impressed. "How'd you do that?"

"You just have to be prepared," Dawn said, picking out the hoof quickly and then putting it down. "Come try the other front foot and I'll talk you through it."

She leaned over her cousin's shoulder as Luna reached tentatively for the horse's other front hoof. It took a few tries, but Luna finally got the mare's foot cleaned out.

It was only after all four hooves were clean that Dawn realized she hadn't even thought about the fact that Luna was a zombie or noticed her zombie odor, even though the two girls had been standing very close together.

But she shrugged off the thought. Between her perfume, the usual barn smells, and Luna's riding clothes, maybe it wasn't that strange after all.

The next morning, Dawn glanced in the mirror over her dresser, fiddling with her hair. She was trying to take a little extra time to look her best these days.

"Dawn?" her mother's voice floated up the stairs. "Hurry up! You don't want the Donovans to have to wait for you."

"Coming!" Dawn shouted back.

She paused just long enough to tweak her hair once more and add another spritz of perfume to her throat. Then she grabbed her backpack and headed downstairs.

When she appeared in the kitchen, her father checked his watch. "Good, you should still have time for breakfast," he said. "Toast or cereal?"

"Toast is good." Dawn patted Mr. Marmalade, who barely looked up as he eagerly gobbled his own breakfast. Then she picked up a slice of toast from the plate on the counter and took a bite.

Her mother was bustling around the kitchen, already dressed in her lab coat. She poured a glass of orange juice and set it down in front of Dawn. "So, Dawn, your father and I were just realizing that your birthday is less than two weeks away. How do you want to celebrate this year?"

Dawn chewed slowly, not sure what to say. How could her parents expect her to celebrate a birthday like this one?

"Uh, I don't know," she said, her mood sinking into her shoes. Just when she'd almost managed to forget that her normal life might be over soon, her parents had to go and remind her! "Nothing, I guess."

"Nonsense!" her mother said. "This is an important birthday."

"Angela," Dawn's dad warned, seeming to guess Dawn's thoughts.

Dawn's mother pursed her lips. "I know, I know. But maybe she could take some of her new friends out for pizza down in East Valley on Saturday, the day before her actual birthday. That way . . ."

She let her voice trail off. Dawn kept her gaze on her toast.

"We should let Dawn decide," her father said. "Maybe it would be better to stick to a family party right here in Vespertine. The Donovan kids could come, too, if you want, Dawn."

Yeah, great idea. Dawn could just imagine what Jake and Jane would say if they got to witness her turning into a zombie right in front of them!

She caught herself just before some drool escaped her mouth. Sucking the saliva back in, she shot a look at her parents to see if they'd noticed. They weren't looking at Dawn, but that didn't make her feel much better.

"Hello, hello!" a cheerful voice rang out from the front hall. "Anybody home?"

"Back here, Nancy!" Dawn's mother called out.

Dr. Nancy lived less than a block away, so she and Dawn's mom carpooled to work. Usually, when the zombie scientist arrived, Mr. Marmalade made himself scarce. Today, though, he remained crouched by his food bowl when she hurried in.

"Greetings, Romeros," Dr. Nancy said cheerfully, helping herself to a slice of toast.

Dawn watched Mr. Marmalade out of the corner of her eye. The cat bristled briefly, then took another bite of food before sidling out of the room.

"Check it out," Dawn said. "I think Mr. Marmalade's getting used to zombies. I told you it wasn't a mistake to bring him with us."

Her mother traded smiles with Dr. Nancy. "I suppose you're right," Mrs. Romero said. "It just goes to show that anyone can adjust to just about anything."

"Whatever." Dawn cleared a little more excess saliva out of her throat, then slung her backpack over one shoulder. "I'd better go or I'll be late."

Chapter Eleven

Dawn and the twins were the first ones to their usual
lunch table that day. It was taco salad day, and the
others were all in line to buy lunch.

"You okay, Dawn?" Jake tossed his lunch bag
onto the table. "You've been kind of quiet today."

Dawn's heart jumped. She always noticed everything about Jake; was he starting to notice stuff
about her, too? The thought was a little scary, but
mostly exciting.

Then Dawn remembered why she'd been quiet,
and she sighed. For a second, she didn't want to talk
about it. Then she realized the twins were probably
the only people who might understand how she was
feeling. And this could be her best chance to talk to
them in private.

"It's my parents." Dawn shot a look around the cafeteria to make sure nobody else was close enough to hear. "They started talking about my birthday this morning. Like wanting to celebrate it and saying what a big, important birthday this is . . ." She made a face.

"So what?" Jane pulled a container of pretzels out of her bag. "I know people in Vespertine are all weird about turning thirteen, for obvious reasons." She rolled her eyes.

"Yeah, but we don't have to worry about that, right?" Jake said. "So if they're offering you a big party or something, take it! We'll be there, right, Jane?"

"Definitely," Jane said, but then frowned. "Especially since our dad is being totally lame about *our* birthday."

"I thought he bought you guys all kinds of cool stuff when you went into town last weekend," Dawn said.

"He did." Jane was still unpacking her lunch bag. She set a bottle of juice and a sandwich next to the pretzels. "But he's refusing to do anything to celebrate our birthday on Thursday. Says he has some kind of huge work deadline."

"Yeah, it's kind of weird, actually." Jake looked up from his food. "Usually, he's all about our birthday. Like last year — he let us take the day off school to go to the circus." He shrugged. "But it's no biggie, really. Jane's just being dramatic as usual. Dad said we can do anything we want over the weekend after his deadline's done."

"I am *not* dramatic!" Jane told her brother dramatically. "Anyway, I think Dad should make up for his lameness by taking us out somewhere extra good this year."

"Like where?" Jake said.

"Maybe he'll fly you guys to New York City," Dawn put in. Whatever the twins ended up doing for their birthday, would they invite her along? She hoped so. It might be the last chance she got to do something fun and normal before her own birthday the following weekend.

"Maybe." Jane sounded like she was only half joking. "Or we could go to that fancy new French restaurant over in River City."

"French food? No, thanks." Jake made a face. "But speaking of River City, we could catch a baseball game there. Oh! Or there's always rock climbing . . ."

They were still arguing about it when Xander, Yasmin, and Zack arrived. "What are you guys talking about?" Xander asked as he set down his tray.

"Nothing," Jake said quickly. "So what'd you guys do this weekend?"

Yasmin flopped down between Jane and Zack. "I watched a documentary with my sister last night," she announced. "It was about the history of environmental protests."

Zack made a face. "Thrilling. I watched a zombie movie marathon myself." He held his arms out in front of him, almost knocking over Xander's drink. "Bra-a-a-ains!" he moaned.

Dawn froze, not sure how to respond. But Jake just laughed. "Yeah, I caught part of that, too," he said. "So, Yas, did you get all inspired to run out and protest against global warming?"

"Sort of." Yasmin carefully unfolded her paper napkin and set it in her lap. "Actually, it gave me a cool idea. We should protest the Z Corp lab!"

"No way," Zack said. "I don't want to get too close to that place. I like the number of fingers and noses I have already."

"I'm serious," Yasmin said. "For all we know, that place might be poisoning the air and water supply even down here in East Valley! Not to mention all the innocent woodland creatures that could be deformed or dying up on the mountain." She sounded more excited with every word. "It's not right! We can't let them get away with it!"

"Okay," Xander said. "So how does it work? Do we just, like, go up there and wave signs around?"

Dawn traded an anxious look with Jake. If the kids from East Valley went up to Z Corp to protest, the zombies' secret would be in danger! Besides, her mother worked at Z Corp. Dawn was sure the lab didn't do any of the bad stuff the other kids were talking about.

"Sounds kind of lame." Jane spoke up before either of them could say anything. She was picking at her sandwich, looking completely bored. "So does anyone know if we're having a social studies quiz this week?"

Yasmin didn't even seem to hear her. "It doesn't have to be just signs," she said. "One of the pro-testers in the movie wanted to raise awareness about, like, animal rights or something. So he took a bunch of red paint and splashed it all over the windows of this pet store. It was supposed to look like blood."

"Cool." Zack sounded interested now. "Maybe we should do something like that."

"Yeah!" Yasmin's eyes flashed, and she waved one of her carrot sticks. "We could splash red paint all over the windows of Z Corp to show how they have, like, all this blood on their hands."

"Wait," Dawn said. "You can't do that."

All three East Valley kids turned to look at her. "Why not?" Xander asked.

"Well, it's all only rumors about Z Corp . . ." Dawn began. But before she could continue her argument, she realized saliva was building up in her mouth. She clamped it shut and swallowed back the drool, almost choking.

Luckily, Jake jumped in. "Also, couldn't we get in trouble for, like, vandalism or something?" he said. "I don't know about you, but I don't want to be grounded for the rest of my life."

"He has a point," Xander agreed. "If we're going to protest, maybe we should just do the sign thing."

Dawn was relieved. She traded a quick look with Jane, who just shrugged.

"Boring." But Zack looked slightly worried now, too. Suddenly, his eyes lit up. "Wait, I know! How about we t.p. the place?"

"Huh?" Dawn said.

"You know — get a bunch of toilet paper and wrap the whole place in it." Zack grinned. "People do that at Halloween all the time, and nobody gets busted for vandalism."

"I like it!" Yasmin smiled. "It will let them know we're watching them."

Xander pumped his fist. "Yeah, that'll teach those weirdos!" He shot Dawn and the twins a glance. "Um, no offense," he added quickly. "I just mean the weirdos at Z Corp, not the rest of you weirdos."

Once again, Dawn wanted to try to change their minds before it was too late. But once again, she could feel a mouthful of drool building up.

As she stopped to swallow again, Jane laughed. "No offense taken," she said. "We can show you the best way to sneak over there through the woods. Right, guys?"

"Sure," Jake agreed. All Dawn could do was gulp and nod. For a second her mind flashed to that scary zombie woman, but of course she couldn't say anything about that in front of the others.

"Awesome!" Yasmin said. "We'll do it this Friday night."

As the other kids started eagerly planning their adventure, Jake leaned toward Dawn. "It's okay," he whispered just loudly enough for her to hear. "If we go through the woods, they'll never even get near the town. And we'll make sure it's late, after everyone at the lab has gone home."

Dawn just nodded again, not quite trusting herself to speak yet as she swallowed down more drool. Maybe Jake was right. The East Valley kids would probably just t.p. a few trees and bushes and then run away. If Dawn and the twins were careful, there was no way anyone would see anything they shouldn't.

It was no big deal. Right?

Chapter Twelve

On Wednesday night, Dawn lounged on her bed, reading a battered copy of *Huckleberry Finn*. They were having a test on it in a couple of weeks, and she wanted to be ready.

Of course, that's only if I'm still going to VCJH in a couple of weeks, Dawn thought.

She glanced at the calendar hanging on the bulletin board above her desk. Her thirteenth birthday was marked out in bright pink highlighter. She'd done that when she first got the calendar last fall, before she found out just how important her next birthday really was.

Dawn sighed and patted Mr. Marmalade, who was dozing on her pillow. She flipped to the next page in the book but couldn't seem to focus on the words. Her mind kept sliding back to the Z Corp prank. She'd hoped the East Valley kids would lose interest before it actually happened, but two days later, they seemed more excited about it than ever.

Dawn closed her eyes, thinking over what she'd discussed with the twins. A little toilet paper wouldn't hurt anyone. She and the twins would be there to make sure things didn't go any further than that. The twins had detailed their plan for how to go through the woods and avoid the town completely, and then they could sneak right back out afterward. As for that scary zombie woman, she probably wouldn't dare to attack a whole group of people. No problem.

"Dawn!" her father shouted from downstairs. "Dinner!"

Dawn opened her eyes and sat up, dog-earing her page. She'd read barely half a chapter, but her homework would have to wait. Her relatives were coming to dinner that night, and Dawn knew she'd better not be late.

"Coming!" she yelled back — or tried to, anyway. A wad of phlegm caught in her throat, making her cough and hack.

Startled, Mr. Marmalade jumped to his feet. He eyed Dawn warily as she spit excess saliva into her trash can.

"It's okay, boy," she choked out, reaching for the cat.

But Mr. Marmalade dodged her and jumped off the bed, disappearing through the half-open door. Dawn coughed again, then frowned and glanced at the calendar once more. Her birthday was only eleven days away now, and her symptoms seemed to be getting worse. Was she kidding herself by still holding out hope that nothing would happen on the big day? She already knew she had a seventy-five percent chance of turning, and the constant flow of saliva in her mouth seemed to be telling her it was even higher than that. Maybe she should forget about her plans to talk her parents into moving back to their old hometown, and instead focus on figuring out how she was going to deal with her new zombie life.

She shuddered. "No," she whispered, heading for the door. As long as there was any hope at all, she was going to stay positive. Or at least try.

Downstairs, Dawn found that her relatives had already arrived. Uncle Charlie and Gram were over by the stove, watching Dawn's father carve a large roast.

Gramps and Dawn's mother were making a salad for the non-zombies in the group. Aunt Kim was peering at the cookbooks on the shelf over the microwave. Everyone was talking and laughing, and the scent of roasted meat mingled with the faint odor of zombies.

But Dawn barely glanced at the adults. Her attention went straight to her cousin. Luna was sitting at the kitchen table — with Mr. Marmalade kneading biscuits as he settled into her lap!

"Wow," Dawn said, staring at the cat. "He's really gotten used to you guys."

Luna smiled up at her. "I bribed him with a piece of beef fat," she said. "Now we're BFFs."

Dawn's mother glanced over. "Oh, good, you're here," she said to Dawn. "Can you and Luna set the table in the dining room, please? The food will be ready in a sec."

"Sure," Dawn said, still staring at her cat. Nobody ever could have guessed he'd been terrified of zombies just a couple of weeks earlier.

"No problem, Aunt Angela." Luna scratched Mr. Marmalade under the chin, then gently deposited him on the floor.

Dawn led the way into the dining room, which was at the other end of a short hallway that also opened into the pantry and a powder room. Mr. Marmalade wandered along after the two girls, purring loudly.

"I'll do silverware and napkins if you do plates and glasses," Luna offered.

"Deal." Dawn opened the cabinet and pulled out a stack of plates. She set them out slowly, still thinking about the stupid prank on Z Corp.

She was so distracted that she almost bumped into her cousin, who was arranging flatware beside one of the plates. "Watch where you're going — I'm armed, you know." Luna laughed and held up a butter knife.

"Sorry," Dawn muttered.

Luna peered at her. "You okay? You look kind of — I don't know, weird."

She looked weird? Dawn grimaced, taking in her cousin's green skin. But she immediately felt guilty for that kind of reaction. She could almost hear her parents' voices in her head: *Zombies are people, too!*

"It's nothing," she said quickly, hoping Luna hadn't guessed her thoughts. "It's just, um . . ." She glanced toward the kitchen. It was too far away for the adults to hear them talking. "These kids at school were talking about sneaking up here and messing around. You know, just because they think Vespertine is weird."

She expected her cousin to be upset. Instead, Luna just rolled her eyes.

"Yeah, that happens every so often," Luna said. "Usually around Halloween, or when someone down there starts a new crazy rumor about us." She shrugged. "It's no big deal."

"It's not?" Dawn was surprised.

Luna smiled. "It always goes the same way, pretty much. The normals try to sneak in and pull something, but Mrs. Tompkins sees them. Or her dog hears them — he sleeps right by the door and hears everything." She straightened a fork. "They sound the alarm, most of us get out of sight, and the police send a few non-expressed officers to escort the outsiders out of town."

"Oh." Dawn hesitated, wondering if she should tell her cousin the rest. Especially the part about how she and the twins were supposed to help the other kids sneak in through the woods. They wouldn't need to pass Mrs. Tompkins's house that way, which meant she wouldn't know to sound the alarm.

But so what? Dawn had been telling herself that the prank wouldn't cause any real harm. She and the twins would be there to make sure of that. What if something went wrong, though? What if the East Valley kids peeked in and saw that zombie statue in the Z Corp lobby? Or the charts in the labs? What if they ran into a real live zombie out for a moonlight stroll — maybe even that weird, scary zombie woman who kept attacking Dawn?

What would happen to Vespertine then?

Luna folded a napkin and put it down beside the plate Dawn had just set out. "Anyway, if you're worried, you could let Mrs. T know to keep an extra-close lookout." She laughed. "But she probably won't even need it."

Before Dawn could decide whether to say anything else, the sound of footsteps came from the hallway. A moment later, her father burst in, carrying the roast. The rest of the family was right behind him.

"Hope you're hungry, girls," Mr. Romero sang out. "There's plenty of meat here for everyone." His gaze fell on Dawn. "Don't worry, kiddo, there's plenty of salad, too."

For a second, Dawn wasn't sure what he was talking about. Then she remembered — she'd told him at the diner that she was thinking of going vegetarian.

Now that she thought about it, he'd been cooking up tasty vegetarian meals every night since then. She realized he was probably trying to be extra nice and make sure she got a chance to enjoy all her favorite fruits, veggies, and grains before she had to stop eating them forever.

"It's okay." Dawn quickly set out the last few glasses. "Um, I decided not to go totally vegetarian after all."

"Really? Well, that's good, because you wouldn't want to miss this roast." Her father grinned and set it in the middle of the table. "Come on, everybody, let's eat!"

On Thursday morning, Dawn didn't have an appetite. She couldn't do much more than stir her cereal around in the bowl while she worried over what to do about the prank. Staring down at the banana slices floating in the milk, she couldn't help noticing they looked like tiny bald zombie heads. Only not green.

She shuddered and pushed the bowl away. Her father looked up from his copy of the weekly *Vespertine Times.*

"Your cereal okay, kiddo?" he asked. "I could make French toast or something if you'd rather. You've still got plenty of time."

"No, thanks, I'm not that hungry." Dawn was glad her mother had left early for the lab. She loved to quote all the scientific research about breakfast being the most important meal of the day. "Um, I think I'll just head over to the Donovans' now."

She dumped her cereal into the sink, then grabbed her backpack. There was no way she could survive two more days of worrying. She needed to talk to someone, and luckily she knew the perfect someone. Some*ones*, actually. If she could get over to the twins' house before their father was ready to leave, maybe they could help her figure out a plan. She could only hope they wouldn't think she was a snitch or a poor sport for wanting to stop the prank. . . .

The phone rang, startling her out of her thoughts. Her dad stood and picked up the old-fashioned land-line handset.

"Hello?" he said.

Dawn waved and headed for the door, figuring it was probably her mother. Who else would be calling this early?

But her father motioned for her to wait. "Yes, I see," he said into the phone. "No, it's all right, I understand. Thanks for letting us know."

He hung up. "Who was that?" Dawn asked.

"Mr. Donovan. It seems the twins caught some kind of nasty bug. They won't be going to school today." Her father tossed the paper aside and glanced down at his robe and slippers. "Guess I'll have to drive you down."

"Oh. That stinks." Dawn sniffled, automatically sucking back the extra saliva that always seemed to be in her mouth now. She was sorry to hear the twins were sick. But maybe there was a silver lining. It was already Thursday, so Jake and Jane probably wouldn't go to school tomorrow, either. The other kids might want to put off the prank until the twins could be there. That would give her more time to figure out what to do.

By the time she got home from school that day, Dawn was feeling much more optimistic about things. She'd had no trouble at all convincing the East Valley kids to postpone the prank until the following Friday. Now all she had to do was figure out how to convince Jake and Jane to help her talk them out of it before then.

"I'm going next door," she told her dad as he dropped the car keys on the bench in the front hall. "I picked up homework for Jake and Jane in case they're still sick tomorrow."

"Okay." Her father headed for the kitchen. "Just make sure you don't catch whatever they've got. No sharing sodas, and definitely no kissing, got it?" He glanced back over his shoulder, winking to show he was kidding around.

Dawn smiled quickly and turned away before he could see her cheeks go red. Why had her mind jumped right to Jake when her father mentioned kissing?

She pushed that out of her mind as she walked next door. The Donovans' house was quiet, and the curtains were drawn in the front room. Dawn knocked tentatively.

It took three more knocks before the door finally opened. Mr. Donovan was standing there in sweats and worn-out bedroom slippers, his hair disheveled. His face was always pale, but today it seemed to float like a ghost's against the dark room behind him.

"Dawn," he said, seeming vaguely surprised to see her. "Hello."

"Hi." Dawn held up the folder of homework she'd brought. "How are the twins? I brought their homework so they won't get behind while they're sick."

Mr. Donovan smiled faintly. "Thank you, Dawn; that was very thoughtful. But they won't be needing those assignments."

Dawn blinked at him. "What do you mean?"

"The twins won't be returning to school," Mr. Donovan explained. "Not to VCJH, at least."

"What? Why not?" Dawn asked.

Mr. Donovan opened his mouth, then closed it again. "Well . . ." he began.

"Just tell her, Dad." A bitter voice came from farther inside the darkened house. It sounded raspy but familiar. "She'll find out soon anyway."

"Jake?" Dawn called. "Is that you?"

"It's me."

Jake stepped into view. He was a zombie!

Chapter Thirteen

Dawn gasped, stumbling back and almost falling off the front step. "What — how —" she stammered.

"Yeah, if you think *you're* surprised . . ." Jake rolled his eyes, which were bloodred, other than the iris and pupil. "Happy birthday to me, right?"

Dawn couldn't do anything but stare for a moment. Jake's skin looked like moldy mayonnaise. His hair had come out in tufts. His left shoulder hunched up, making him look lopsided. Zombie smell wafted off him.

Even while Dawn's mouth still hung open in shock, her logical mind had already worked out what had happened. He'd changed. And not mildly like Luna, either. He was even worse than Gram or Uncle Charlie.

How could I have forgotten it was his birthday today? she thought. *I mean* their *birthday . . .*

"Jane?" she choked out.

Jake nodded. "She's zombied out, too. Pretty crazy that we were both in that unlucky two percent, huh?" He glared at his father, who was still standing there hanging on to the door frame.

"Jake . . ." Mr. Donovan began softly.

Jake ignored him. "So anyway, you probably want to get away as fast as possible," he told Dawn with a frown. "Don't worry, I totally understand. It's —" He hesitated for a second. "It's been nice knowing you."

Dawn swallowed hard, and for once, it wasn't because of extra phlegm. He was right. She wanted to run away and never look back. She wanted to forget she'd ever seen Jake like this. Especially when she thought about her own birthday coming up a week from Sunday. Would she end up the same way?

"Jake! Don't be rude." Mr. Donovan finally seemed to wake up from his daze. "I'm sure Dawn doesn't feel that way. It's not as if you're the first expressed zombie she's ever met. Would you like to come in, Dawn?"

Dawn hesitated for only a second. Jake was watching her, and she didn't want to hurt his feelings.

"Sure, thanks." She stepped inside, glad her perfume hadn't worn off yet. Zombie smells didn't bother her that much anymore, but Jake's was pretty strong.

"Well," Mr. Donovan said faintly. "I've got work to do, so . . ."

His voice drifted off as he hurried out of the room, leaving Dawn alone with Jake. Jake stared at her, a hint of suspicion in his eyes. But there was something else, too. Relief? She wasn't sure. She didn't like staring too long into those red-rimmed eyes.

"Um, so where's Jane?" she asked.

"Hiding in her room. She's not taking this well. As you probably could've guessed." A ghost of a smile flitted across Jake's green-mottled face. "Come on, let's see if we can get her to come out."

At first Jane refused to let Dawn see her. It took almost ten straight minutes of Jake pounding on her door before she finally swung it open.

"Fine!" she exclaimed, glaring at Dawn and Jake. "If you want to see how hideous I am, help yourself."

Dawn tried not to let her shock show. Jane looked just as bad as her twin. "You don't look that bad," she lied. "I mean, it's not like you two are the only zombies I've ever seen, right?"

Jake chuckled politely, but Jane scowled. "Don't use that word," she snapped.

"What, zombie?" Jake rolled his eyes. "Get real. It's what we are, okay? So deal with it."

"Shut up." Jane glared at him.

As drool dripped down Jane's chin, Dawn realized saliva was building up again in her own mouth. She swallowed it quickly.

"Um — so was your dad surprised?" she asked, not sure what else to say. She wanted to ask how it felt, how exactly it had happened. But she didn't quite dare. She wasn't sure the twins were ready to talk about that.

"I don't know. Sort of." Jake shrugged, though the motion looked strange with his newly hunched shoulder. "But he admitted our percentages weren't as low as we always thought. Turns out our mom did have some zombie blood after all."

"Really?" Dawn glanced at Jane, who was staring at the floor. "Wow, that's crazy."

"Yeah." Jake picked at the hem of his shirt.

"Just goes to show, you never know." Jane glanced at Dawn. "We thought we had a super-low percentage. Surprise!" She grimaced, allowing a trickle of drool to escape. "You probably shouldn't assume you're safe, either. Especially after the way your parents didn't tell you the truth until a few months ago. Who knows if they told the truth about your percentage, either, right?"

Jake frowned at his sister. "Don't take it out on Dawn. She's not going to turn like we did."

Dawn wanted to tell them the truth about her percentage. At least she *knew* she had a high chance of turning next weekend. The twins had been sure they were safe. They'd been totally blindsided. But would telling them now make the twins feel better — or worse?

Not the right moment, she told herself. *This is about them, not me.* It was obvious how shocked and miserable the twins were, which made her feel sorry for them. But then, Dawn still wasn't sure what to say to them, and they all just ended up sitting around awkwardly for a while.

A clock somewhere in the house struck four o'clock. Suddenly, Dawn remembered something, and relief flooded through her. "Oh," she said. "I'm supposed to be meeting Luna outside right now. We have a riding lesson." She stood up. "So I should go. Sorry."

"It's okay." Jake smiled weakly. "Thanks for coming over."

Dawn headed for the door. "Sure. Happy birthday." She winced and shot them a look. "Um, you know."

"Yeah," Jake said softly as Jane rolled her red-veined eyes. "See you later."

"See you." Dawn took a deep breath as she escaped from the house. That had been seriously uncomfortable.

But she would have to think about it later. She could see Luna waiting outside her house.

Dawn was pretty busy for the next week. So busy she didn't have time to stop in and see the twins. At least that was what she told herself.

She thought about them every time she saw their house, though. And every time her father grumbled about driving her all the way down to East Valley for school.

"Let's go," he said on Friday morning, swiping his keys off the bench. "You're going to be late if we don't leave now."

"Coming." Dawn glanced over at the Donovan house as she hurried toward the car. What were the twins doing right now? What had they been doing all week? She knew from talking to Luna that they hadn't turned up at Vespertine Academy yet. And they *definitely* weren't showing their new faces down in East Valley. Everyone there thought they had mono.

Dawn shuddered, turning away from their house and hurrying to the car. Her own thirteenth birthday was on Sunday, just two days away now. Was she going to be like the twins soon?

She ended up stumbling through her morning classes in a daze. By the time she entered the cafeteria, she'd figured out exactly how many hours, seconds, and minutes were left before she turned thirteen and discovered her fate.

"Dawn! Hurry up!" Zack spotted her coming and waved. Yasmin and Xander waved, too.

For a second, Dawn wasn't sure why they all looked so excited. Then she remembered with a feeling of dread: It was the day of the prank. She'd been so distracted by the twins' surprise change that she'd almost forgotten about it.

"Are you psyched?" Yasmin asked, grabbing Dawn's arm. "This is going to be epic!"

Xander grinned. "My mom almost caught me leaving with eight rolls of toilet paper," he said. "I had to pretend to spot a bald eagle at the bird feeder to distract her long enough to get out of the house."

The others laughed loudly. Dawn could barely crack a smile. "This just doesn't feel the same without the twins," she said. "Maybe we should —"

"I meant to ask you about them," Zack interrupted. "You live right next door, right? Have you seen them?"

"Yeah, how are they doing?" Yasmin put in. "I e-mailed Jane, but she never wrote back."

"Um, I don't know." Dawn shrugged and busied herself unwrapping her sandwich. "I mean, I heard they're really sick, so they're probably not up to e-mailing and stuff."

"Oh." Yasmin took a sip of her juice. "Anyway, listen. Where should we meet up with you tonight? My sister said she'd drive the three of us up there." She gestured vaguely in the direction of the mountain.

"I know," Zack said. "We could meet by that weird stone sign. Have you guys seen it?"

Xander nodded. "Great idea. It's far enough outside of town that nobody will see us."

Yasmin glanced at Dawn. "What do you think? Is it close enough to walk to Z Corp from there?"

"Um . . ." Dawn sniffled and chewed her lower lip, trying to work up the courage to say she didn't want to do it. Could she pretend to not know the way through the woods by herself? It wouldn't be that much of a stretch — she wasn't extremely familiar with the woods. Then again, letting them go alone might be worse. . . . Suddenly, she noticed Xander staring at her and felt a stab of panic. Xander was pretty smart. Had he figured out what she was hiding? "What?" she asked.

"I hope you didn't catch mono from the twins," he said, scooting his chair a little farther away from Dawn's. "You sound really stuffed up right now."

"I do?" Dawn cleared her throat, realizing the phlegm and saliva had built up again. Was she getting so accustomed to drooling that she didn't even notice it anymore? "Um, it's probably just allergies."

She bent over her food, pretending to be totally focused on picking the poppy seeds off her bagel. Her birthday was only two days away, and the drooling symptoms were worse than ever. After seeing what had happened to Jake and Jane, there was no way she could avoid the truth: She was becoming a zombie.

The thought distracted her so much that she never quite got around to backing out of the prank.

When the bell rang to end lunch period, Yasmin jumped out of her seat. "See you tonight by the sign, Dawn!"

Dawn opened her mouth, searching for the words to say she was out. But it was too late. The others were already gone.

Chapter Fourteen

"Out you go, kiddo." Dawn's dad stopped the car in front of their house. "I've got to go pick up a few things at the store."

"Thanks for the ride, Dad." Dawn waved as her father drove off.

When she turned to go inside, her gaze fell on the house next door. Suddenly, she realized she hadn't spoken to the twins in over a week. She realized something else, too. She missed them.

After dropping her backpack on her front step, she headed over. Jake answered the door.

"Oh," he said, his mottled green face blank. "It's you."

"Hi." Dawn took a deep breath and managed a

small smile. "Sorry I haven't been around much. School's been busy, and . . ."

Her voice trailed off as Jane appeared behind her brother. "What are you doing here?" Jane demanded. "We figured you decided you were too good to hang out with zombies like us."

"It's not that," Dawn protested. "I mean, yeah, it was kind of a shock. But I definitely still want to be friends with you guys."

Jake folded his arms over his chest. "You have a funny way of showing it. Seriously, we thought you bolted."

Dawn took a deep breath and blurted out the truth. "I was scared, okay?"

"Scared of what? Zombies?" Jane wrinkled her nose. "Get real."

"Not scared of zombies." Dawn clutched the railing of their front steps. "Scared of *becoming* a zombie. When I see you guys like this, it's hard to not think about becoming one myself. I was afraid to face up to that."

Jake looked confused. "But why are you so worried about that? Just because our percentages turned out to be wrong doesn't mean you have any more chance of turning than you always thought."

"That's the thing." Dawn knew this was going to be the hardest part. "I, um, didn't exactly tell you guys the truth about my percentage."

Jane narrowed her eyes. "What do you mean?"

"I don't have a two percent chance or whatever. I have a — a seventy-five percent chance."

Both twins gasped. "What?" Jake exclaimed.

"I'm sorry, I shouldn't have lied." Dawn swallowed back a mouthful of saliva. "But I was afraid to tell you guys before. You talked a lot about your low percentage, and how you couldn't wait to get out of Vespertine and stuff." She shrugged. "I figured you might not want to be friends if you knew I'd probably be a zombie soon. I guess that's stupid, but I didn't really think it through at the time, you know?"

The twins looked at each other. There was a long moment of silence. Dawn held her breath. Would they forgive her?

Finally, Jake sighed. "No, I get it," he said, leaning back against the door frame. "I guess we kind of sounded like anti-zombie snobs before, didn't we."

It didn't really sound like a question, but Dawn nodded. "Maybe a little."

Jane wiped some drool away, then shrugged. "Yeah, sorry about that." She sounded a little bitter. But she flashed Dawn a wry smile. "Guess we learned our lesson, huh?"

"I hope the kids at zombie school will forgive us," Jake added. "Um, I mean Vespertine Academy."

"You guys are going there?" Dawn asked.

Jane settled on the top step, wrapping her arms around her knees. "Our dad gave us a week off to adjust, but he wants us to start next week."

"Hey, silver lining." Jake smiled at Dawn. "At least now all three of us can go there together."

"Yeah." Dawn realized that *was* a silver lining. All along, the worst thing about the idea of going zombie had been the thought of losing the twins as friends.

Well, okay, maybe not the *worst* thing. But definitely top ten.

"So what's been going on at school this week?" Jane sounded wistful. "Does everyone believe we have mono?"

"That's what Dad says he told the school," Jake added.

"Everyone believes it." Dawn hesitated. "By the way, we postponed the prank. It's tonight."

Jane's eyes lit up. "I almost forgot about that! I wish I could still go."

"Not me." Jake looked troubled. "It actually doesn't seem like such a good idea to me anymore."

"Yeah." Dawn smiled at him, glad they were on the same wavelength. Being a zombie hadn't changed Jake except on the outside. He was still one of the coolest people she knew.

"So are you sure you want to go through with it, Dawn?" he asked.

"No. I've never been sure about it," Dawn answered honestly, picking at a peeling flake of paint on the railing. "The others think I'm meeting them at the town sign tonight. But I'm sort of thinking about doing a no-show." That was the only solution that had occurred to her on the ride home from school. Maybe if she didn't turn up to guide them through the woods, the others would give up and go home.

"Probably not a good idea," Jake said slowly. "What if they come into town looking for you?"

Jane shrugged. "So what? Mrs. Tompkins would spot them."

"I guess." But Jake still looked worried.

They discussed it until Dawn spotted her father's car turning onto their block. "Listen, I should go," she said reluctantly.

Jake smirked. "Uh-oh. She's bolting again!"

"No way." Dawn crossed her heart with one finger. "You guys can't get rid of me that easily."

"Cool." Jane smiled. "Let us know what you decide to do tonight, okay?"

"Definitely." Dawn smiled back. She realized that she already wasn't bothered by their new zombie appearances.

"See you." Jake reached over and touched Dawn's arm.

"See you," Dawn said — but though she didn't mind his looks, she couldn't help shuddering at the feel of his greenish, slightly slimy fingers.

Jake quickly pulled his hand away, tucking it behind his back. Was that hurt in his red-rimmed eyes?

"Have a good birthday on Sunday," he said quietly. "Maybe we can hang out *after* that."

Dawn bit her lip, wishing she could take back that shudder. But the twins were already going back inside.

Anyway, Jake was right. After Sunday, everything would be different.

* * *

Dawn stared at the glowing blue numbers on her alarm clock. It was twenty minutes to eleven. If she was going to meet the other kids at the town sign, she had to leave now.

Mr. Marmalade was sleeping on her legs. He woke up when she slid them out from under him.

"Shh!" she warned when he meowed. "I've got to go."

Her heart pounded and she clutched the edge of her sheet as she thought about her options one more time. The first option was the most tempting. She could just not show up. After all, she'd probably be turning into a zombie on Sunday, which meant she'd never see Xander, Yasmin, or Zack again.

But, as Jake had said, if Dawn didn't show up, the East Valley kids might wander into Vespertine looking for her. What if Mrs. Tompkins missed them just this once? What if the kids saw something they shouldn't? Dawn didn't like to think about what might happen then.

Another option was to tell her parents what was going on, or maybe the Vespertine police. But that didn't seem like much of a plan, either. She didn't want to get the East Valley kids in trouble; they were her friends, even if she never saw them again. Besides, she knew they didn't mean any real harm with their prank. And it wasn't like she could tell them what was really going on at Z Corp.

Dawn swung her legs over the edge of the bed and stood up. There was only one option left: She had to go through with the prank. She didn't like the thought of messing up the lab, but at least it was just a little toilet paper. Maybe she could even volunteer to help clean it up tomorrow.

"Here I go," she whispered, giving Mr. Marmalade one last pat. She grabbed the flashlight out of her desk drawer on her way out of the room.

There were definitely advantages to being a good kid all her life. Dawn had no trouble at all sneaking out of the house. Soon, she was wheeling her bike toward the sidewalk. Thick clouds hid the light of the nearly full moon, and it was hard to see more than two feet in front of her.

She'd just swung her leg over the bike when two zombies materialized out of the darkness. Dawn almost screamed but swallowed it back just in time.

"Shh! It's just us," a familiar voice whispered.

"Jake?" Dawn peered at the zombies. "Jane? What are you guys doing out here?" Both twins were dressed in dark clothes and were holding their bikes.

"We decided we couldn't miss out on the fun," Jane whispered with a smirk.

"Actually, we realized it's sort of our fault you're stuck doing it," Jake added. "We feel bad, and we wanted to be around for moral support."

"But the others . . ." Dawn could only imagine what the East Valley kids would say if they saw the twins in their current state.

"Don't worry, we'll stay out of sight," Jane said. "We can hide in the woods and watch."

Her voice didn't sound sarcastic anymore. It sounded kind of sad. For a second, Dawn wasn't sure why.

Then she figured it out. Jane probably missed her friends from VCJH. This might be her last chance to catch a glimpse of them.

"Okay, let's go," Dawn said. Having the twins along made her feel a little better. "Might as well get it over with."

The three of them biked across town. When they passed Mrs. Tompkins's, her little mop dog started barking inside the house. Dawn and the twins quickly hid behind a bush across the road.

"Why's that fluffball barking at us?" Jane whispered.

Dawn just shook her head, afraid to speak. A second later, the door opened. Mrs. Tompkins peered out with her usual suspicious look. Her dog raced out onto the porch and sniffed the air.

"What is it, baby?" The old woman's voice floated toward the kids in the still, silent night air. "I don't hear anything."

The dog's nose twitched. For a second, Dawn was sure it was staring right at her. Then it barked once more and sauntered back inside.

"I guess he smelled that we're all locals," Jake whispered. "Come on, let's get out of here!"

A few minutes later, they reached the last curve in the road before the town sign. "Jane and I had better stop here," Jake said quietly. "We'll wait a few minutes, then double back and hide along the way to the lab. We can meet up after it's all over."

"Sounds good." Dawn clutched her handlebars tightly. "I'd better go. It's already eleven o'clock."

There wasn't much chance of meeting any traffic at this time of night, so she coasted right down the center of the hilly road. The moon had come out from behind the clouds, so it was easy to see where she was going. She was moving pretty fast as she rounded the curve, but when she caught a glimpse of the town sign, she hit the brakes so hard she almost upended her bike.

"Dawn!" Yasmin spotted her and waved. "We were just wondering if you were ever going to get here. Check it out — my sister's here, too!"

"Yeah. I can see that." Dawn gulped. Yasmin's sister had brought some friends. At least half a dozen high schoolers were lounging on and around the sign. Most of them were boys, and all of them looked pretty tough.

"Yo, is this the guide?" One of the boys, a broad-shouldered kid in a leather jacket, stepped forward. He was swinging a baseball bat at his side. "It's about time! Let's get this show on the road."

Xander sidled over to Dawn, looking nervous. "We didn't know they were coming," he whispered. "I think they're planning to break into Z Corp!"

Chapter Fifteen

"What?" Dawn whispered, eyeing the older kid's baseball bat.

Zack hurried over, casting an anxious look over his shoulder at the older kids. "We told them about the t.p. plan, and they said that's kid stuff," he whispered. "They think we should *really* teach Z Corp a lesson."

Dawn froze. Now what? That was her Mom's workplace! And worse, if the older kids actually got inside, it wouldn't take them long to figure out it wasn't an ordinary lab. Her mind flashed to the zombie statue in the lobby and the zombie charts on all the walls.

"We can't let them do it!" she hissed. "They'll, um, get us all in big trouble if we get caught!"

"We know." Xander looked miserable. "But trust me, they're not going to listen to us."

Before Dawn could respond, one of the older boys strode toward her. This one had dark hair and a can of spray paint in his hand. "Yasmin says you know your way around up here," he said with a smirk. "So let's get moving and have some fun."

Dawn smiled weakly, but her mind was racing. She couldn't let this happen. The world couldn't discover Vespertine's secrets. Not when Dawn was about to go zombie herself in a little over twenty-four hours!

But that wasn't the only reason she wanted to stop this, she realized. Even if a miracle happened and she didn't change, she still wouldn't want the zombies' secret to get out. She thought about Luna, with her cheerful smile and her love of horses, and about Uncle Charlie, Aunt Kim, and Gram. They were her family, and she didn't want a bunch of nosy outsiders up here harassing them. Or Jake and Jane, either, who were still struggling with their new change. Or Dr. Nancy and the others at the lab. Or any of the other zombies in town — yes, even that obnoxious Johnny O'Malley from the diner.

If the world found out the truth about Vespertine, the peaceful little town would never be the same. And it would be all Dawn's fault. She had to fix this herself.

"Listen," she spoke up, glancing from the boy with the spray paint to the others. "I'm not sure this is a good idea. There might be security at the lab, and —"

"No way," the guy with the baseball bat said. "You're not backing out on us now!"

"Yeah." Yasmin's sister raised a fist. "We can't let that evil corporation poison the wilderness!"

Dawn gulped. Okay, so the older kids weren't going to listen to reason, especially from some twelve-year-old they'd just met. There had to be another way. . . .

"Um, okay, that's fine," she blurted out as a new plan popped into her head. "But listen, I just realized I dropped my — my flashlight. Come to think of it, I think I heard it fall right before I got here. I'll be right back."

"Wait." The kid with the spray paint stepped forward. His eyes glinted with suspicion in the moonlight as he grabbed the handlebars of Dawn's bike. "If it's that close, you can walk back and get it."

"Yeah." The baseball-bat guy snorted with laughter. "Don't want you taking off on us now!"

Dawn took a deep breath. "Fine," she said. "I'll be right back."

She hurried off before anyone else could protest. Her legs were shaking so hard, she could barely walk. But she broke into a jog as soon as she rounded the curve.

"Guys?" she hissed, peering into the darkness along the road. "Are you still here?"

For a second, she was afraid it was too late — that Jake and Jane had already left to meet her in the woods near the lab. Then the leaves rustled and Jake stepped into view. Jane was right behind him.

"Dawn?" Jake whispered. "What's going on? Didn't they show up?"

"Oh, they showed up all right. . . ." Dawn quickly told the twins what was happening. "We've got to do something!" she finished. "Can you guys run back and tell Mrs. Tompkins to call the police?"

Jane looked worried. "Won't that get Yas and the others in big trouble?"

"Probably." Dawn bit her lip. "But we can't help that. If those high school kids see anything they shouldn't . . ."

"You're right." Jake nodded. "We've got to stop them, no matter what. It might take a while for the police to get here, though, and the lab isn't that far away from us."

"I'll try to stall them," Dawn promised. She glanced over her shoulder. Was that the sound of someone coming after her? "I've got to go," she hissed. Grabbing her flashlight out of her pocket, she hurried back toward the sign.

"Isn't that the place up ahead?" one of the older kids called out from somewhere behind Dawn on the narrow trail. "How come you want us to go off to the left?"

Dawn glanced forward. The moon was out again, and the Z Corp building was visible rising over the trees, its glass front gleaming in the soft, cool light.

"Um, yeah, that's it." Dawn figured there wasn't much point in lying about that part. "But see, there's this big, really steep ditch between here and there. We have to go around it."

The older kid shrugged, seeming to buy it. "This way, guys!" he called softly to the rest of the group straggling along behind them.

Dawn sneaked a peek at her watch. It had been almost half an hour since they'd started out. She'd led the way as slowly as possible, taking detours she didn't know if she could find the way back from. But now they'd ended up pretty close to the lab. When were the police going to show up?

The group crept down the path to the left. After a few minutes, it dead-ended in a thicket of prickly vines.

"Oops," Dawn said.

"This is bogus," one of the teen boys said, his voice echoing loudly in the dark forest. "We can see the stupid building. Let's just trailblaze our way right to it!"

"Yeah!" one of the other boys agreed. "Here, I'll clear the path."

He started swinging his baseball bat, knocking aside underbrush and small saplings as he charged into the woods.

"Wait!" Dawn called. "Let's just go back to the main trail. We might be able to get through the ditch after all."

Several of the boys looked suspicious, but Yasmin's sister shrugged. "I don't want to fight my way through the woods," she said, smoothing down her long skirt. "Let's try it her way."

"Fine." Baseball-Bat Guy slung his arm around the older girl's shoulders and shot Dawn a wary look. "We'll try it her way. One more time. But we'd better be at that building in ten minutes, or . . ."

He didn't have to say anything more. Dawn gulped, realizing she couldn't stall them much longer.

She kept moving, walking as slowly as she could without raising more suspicion. They would reach the lab in about five minutes. Then what?

Suddenly, something leaped out of the woods right in front of her. "Gaaaargh!" it gurgled.

It was the scary zombie woman! Dawn had almost forgotten about her in all the excitement. The woman's eyes bulged out of her green-mottled face, and spittle flew in every direction.

Dawn screamed at the top of her lungs. She wasn't the only one — the other kids had seen the zombie, too. With shouts of surprise and terror, they all turned and ran.

Dawn did the same. The zombie's woman's extra-strong scent made her gasp for breath as she ran. How close was the zombie? Dawn risked a glance back to see.

At that moment, her foot hit a root on the trail. Dawn went flying, landing flat on her face.

Chapter Sixteen

Dawn flipped herself over, crab-scooting backward as she heard footsteps coming. She glanced over her shoulder, but the other kids were long gone, their shouts fading as they ran away. Dawn's heart pounded with terror as she stared up at the zombie woman. All those movies she'd seen back in the normal world flashed through her mind. What would the zombie woman do to her?

To her surprise, the zombie woman stopped and peered down at Dawn. She waved her hands around and grunted.

"Wuh," she said. "Weeh . . ."

Dawn blinked, sitting up. Was the woman trying to speak? Dawn wasn't sure. But she definitely didn't seem to be trying to eat Dawn's brains.

"Um, what?" Dawn asked uncertainly. "Are — are you trying to say something?"

The woman gurgled, then tried again. It seemed to take vast effort to push the sounds out of her mouth. Dawn listened carefully.

"Meat?" she guessed. "Are you saying meat — are you hungry?'

The woman shook her head and waved her hands, looking angry for a moment. She took a step closer, and Dawn scooted back a little farther.

"Okay, okay, not meat. I get it." She waited for the zombie woman to try again. "Leap?" she guessed next. "Um, reef?" She bit her lip. It was impossible to tell what the woman was trying to say.

The zombie woman took another step. Dawn's muscles tensed, ready to jump up and run.

Then the woman flung something at her. It was a handful of leaves. They fluttered down onto Dawn's stomach.

"Oh," Dawn said. *"Leaf!* Are you saying leaf?" She grabbed the rumpled leaves and held them up.

The zombie woman grunted with excitement, clapping her hands. She pointed at herself, then at the leaves.

Dawn tilted her head, trying to figure out what

the zombie was trying to say. The woman leaned closer, and something that was tangled in her long thicket of dark hair sparkled in the moonlight. Dawn squinted at it in surprise. Could that be . . . ?

"Hey! Anybody here?" a voice shouted.

The zombie woman grunted in surprise, then turned and ran. "Wait!" Dawn called, jumping to her feet. "Come back!"

She started after her. But the zombie had disappeared into the darkness. Dawn wasn't sure which way she'd gone.

A moment later, several people burst into view from the other direction. Jake and Jane were in the lead, with several Vespertine police officers following.

Dawn pointed the police after the East Valley teens. The officers took off immediately, leaving Dawn alone with the twins.

"Are you okay?" Jake asked breathlessly. "We came as fast as we could."

Jane shot an annoyed look after the departing police. "Yeah, it would've been faster except at first the stupid cops thought *we* were the ones trying to pull a prank!"

Dawn waved away their questions and explanations. "Listen, this might sound like a weird thing to ask right now, but what did your mother look like?" She took a deep breath. "And are you absolutely sure she's, um, really dead?"

Jane stared at her. "What?"

"Why are you asking us that?" Jake's face had gone pale in the moonlight.

"Because I just ran into this zombie woman — that's what scared the East Valley kids away." Dawn reached out and touched the charm Jane was wearing around her neck. "She was wearing an earring that looked just like this one."

Jane gasped. "*What?*"

Just then, voices rang out nearby, calling all three of their names. "Uh-oh," Jake muttered. He glanced at Dawn. "Mrs. Tompkins called your parents and our dad. We begged her not to, but . . ."

"That's okay." Dawn bit her lip as she heard her mother's voice. She didn't sound happy. "I guess they would've found out anyway."

"Dawn!" Her father stomped into view. He was wearing rumpled pajama pants with rubber boots and a jacket. "There you are. You have some explaining to do, young lady."

"I know," Dawn said. "But wait, I wasn't done explaining to the twins —"

"It'll have to wait." Her mother sounded even angrier than her father. "We're going home — right now. We'll be having a *long* discussion about this when we get there."

"So your parents weren't mad?" Luna kicked at the ground, sending the swing higher.

Dawn slumped lazily on the swing next to her. "Oh, they were definitely mad at first," she said. "Actually, they pretty much freaked out when Mrs. Tompkins called. But after we got home, we had a long talk about, you know, everything."

Luna nodded sympathetically. "Yeah."

Dawn smiled at her, suddenly feeling lucky to have such a cool cousin. Luna had come over first thing Saturday morning to find out what had happened. Apparently, the whole town was talking about it.

"So what about the twins?" Luna asked. "Is that woman from the woods really their mother?"

"I don't know." Dawn was wondering that herself. "I wanted to go over there right after breakfast, but my parents said it was way too early. They said I had to wait until at least nine A.M."

Luna stopped her swing, grabbed Dawn's wrist,

and checked her watch. Her zombie fingers felt cool and a little slimy, but Dawn barely noticed. "It's five after nine now," Luna said with a smile.

"You're right." Dawn stood up. "Do you mind?"

"Go ahead." Luna started swinging again. "But I want to hear everything later, okay?"

"Promise."

Dawn hurried over to the twins' house. Mr. Donovan answered the door. He smiled when he saw Dawn.

"Ah, here's our favorite neighbor," he said cheerfully, waving her inside. "The twins have been bugging me to let them call you with the news, but I insisted they had to wait until at least nine A.M. to make sure you're not asleep. After all, you were out late last night." He winked.

Dawn just stared at him. He seemed so different! The sad, faraway look in his eyes was gone. Even his clothes looked different — brighter and cleaner. Or maybe they just seemed that way because he was standing up straight and smiling for a change.

Then Jane burst into the room. She rushed over and gave Dawn a hug.

"You were right, it was her!" she exclaimed. "Mom's back!"

Chapter Seventeen

"Really?" Dawn's heart soared. Even after seeing that earring, she hadn't quite dared believe it was true. "That was her out there?"

"Come on." Jane grabbed her hand and tugged on it. "She's in the kitchen!"

Dawn followed Jane and her father as they hurried toward the back of the house. When the three of them entered the kitchen, Jake was digging around inside the refrigerator. Sitting at the table with a cup of coffee was the zombie woman from the woods — the twins' mother.

She looked much better already. Her hair was cut and combed, her skin was green but clean, and her eyes sparkled with intelligence.

"Look, Mom," Jane exclaimed, skipping over. "Dawn's here."

Jake pulled his head out of the fridge. "Hi, Dawn," he said, beaming.

"Hello, Dawn. So you're the girl I kept scaring half to death out in the woods," their mother said with a smile. Her words were slightly garbled, but Dawn had no trouble understanding them. "Sorry about that."

"It's okay." Dawn smiled back, amazed at Mrs. Donovan's transformation. She barely recognized her. "Um, so . . ."

"You're probably wondering what happened last night, right?" Jake wandered over to the table and sat down. "After your parents dragged you off, we told Dad what you said about the earring."

"We didn't think he'd believe us," Jane put in. "But he did."

Mr. Donovan nodded, sinking into the seat beside his wife. "I knew right away that it had to be my Valerie."

"Obviously, she wasn't dead after all." Jane shot her father a slightly sour look.

He sighed. "I'm sorry. I just didn't know how to

tell you kids the truth. You were so young when she . . ." His voice trailed off.

His wife put a hand over his. "It's all right. We're all together now, and that's what matters."

Dawn was still confused. She glanced at Jake, who met her eye. He nodded, seeming to guess what she was thinking.

"When Jane and I were born, Mom was working as a scientist at Z Corp," he explained. "She was a zombie, but very lightly expressed."

His father nodded, squeezing his wife's hand. "We used to travel all the time," he said. "As long as she wore a hat and dark glasses and a bit of makeup, nobody would ever guess she was a zombie."

"Wow," Dawn said. She wondered if she'd seen any lightly expressed zombies herself back in her old life. Somehow, the thought had never occurred to her before.

"Those were the days," the twins' mother said, smiling back at her husband. "All that travel made me realize how small Vespertine is. I wanted my kids to be able to experience the world as I did." She glanced at the twins, her expression loving but sad. "But I knew with our family history, they were almost certain to turn at thirteen."

Mr. Donovan bit his lip. "I'm afraid I lied to them about that part, too. I didn't want them to worry, and of course I couldn't tell them what really happened to their mother. . . ."

"What *did* happen?" Dawn asked. Mrs. Donovan looked a lot better than she had in the woods, but nobody would call her "lightly expressed." Her skin was deeply mottled with green, one shoulder was hunched, and now that her hair was shorter, it was easy to see that chunks of it were missing. Drool oozed continuously from the corner of her mouth, and the whites of her eyes were streaked with dark red veins.

"One of the other scientists came up with a variation of the serum," Mrs. Donovan explained. "Highly experimental, but he hoped it would reduce some of the physical symptoms of the change." She glanced at the twins. "I had to try it — for my babies' sakes. I figured if the new serum made my physical symptoms better, it might help my darling twins avoid them entirely when they were older."

"But instead of reversing her symptoms," her husband put in grimly, "it made them worse."

"Much worse," Mrs. Donovan agreed. "My colleague thought his experimental serum was too dangerous to test on a person yet — he wanted to study it more first. But I couldn't wait. I sneaked in after hours and injected myself with it."

Dawn shivered. "Then what happened?"

"I don't remember things too clearly after that, but from what I gather, the new serum didn't work at all the way it was supposed to. In fact, it canceled out the effects of the regular serum. I became like someone from the early days of Zombie Syndrome, before the serum was developed, when the most severe cases had all sorts of terrible mental symptoms. Aversion to light, loss of speech, terror of humans . . ." Mrs. Donovan ticked the list off on her fingers.

"Wow." That seemed to be all Dawn could say. It was bad enough knowing she might turn into a zombie like the twins or her family members tomorrow. Now she realized she was lucky her fate wasn't even worse. All thanks to the scientists at Z Corp. "So then what happened?"

Mrs. Donovan shrugged. "As I said, I'm not sure. I suppose I thrashed around in the lab until I found the way out. In the process, I must have lost one of my earrings." She touched the squiggle-and-star earring in her left ear, then glanced at the charm on Jane's necklace.

"I found the earring when Dr. Pruitt called to tell me what had happened," Mr. Donovan said. "I kept it, hoping we'd find her. We certainly tried! But she was too wily for us." He smiled wanly. "By the time the kids were old enough to ask about her, I'd just about given up hope. I told them she was dead, figuring that would be easier for them to understand while they were young."

"Yeah." Jane scowled. "And somehow, he never got around to telling us the truth when we got older."

"So you were wandering around out in the woods for years and years, and nobody could track you down?" Dawn said. "So how come I kept running into you?"

Mrs. Donovan laughed. "Good question. As far as I can piece together, I stumbled across a plant out in the woods that I felt interested in eating. Chewing the leaves made my symptoms better — I regained enough of my wits to want to find my way back to the lab, though I wasn't sure why. Or even who I was. Or how to get there. Dawn, you were the first person I encountered after that happened. I suppose I kept trying to find you and express my discovery."

"Wow." That explained a lot. Like why Mrs.

Donovan had kept throwing leaves at her. "Sorry I didn't try harder to understand you."

"It's all right, Dawn." Mrs. Donovan smiled. "You figured out who I was in the end, thank goodness."

Mr. Donovan nodded. "The arrival of the police last night spooked her. But she was still close enough that we were able to find her. Dr. Pruitt and the others came in as soon as I called, and we spent all night carefully dosing her with the serum."

"I still need a few more doses," Mrs. Donovan said, wiping some drool off her chin. "But I already feel almost like myself again. It's good to be home!"

"It's awesome to have you home," Jake said.

Dawn smiled. She could tell that the twins were thrilled at being reunited with their mother. Maybe having a zombie mom around would make it a little easier for them to adjust to their own zombie state.

Jake turned his head and caught her looking at him. He met her gaze with a smile. "We'll never be able to thank you enough, Dawn," he said. "You're a good friend."

"A *great* friend," Jane corrected, reaching over to squeeze Dawn's hand.

"Thanks. You guys are great friends, too," Dawn said.

She realized it was true. The twins were amazing friends. And who knew, maybe someday Jake could be something more. . . .

Feeling herself starting to blush, she cleared her throat, where saliva was building up again. That reminded her that her birthday was tomorrow. This could be her last day as a normal girl. Her happy feelings faded.

"What's wrong?" Jake asked her. "You look sad all of a sudden."

Dawn sighed. "I was just thinking about my birthday."

"She turns thirteen tomorrow," Jane told her parents somberly.

"Oh." Mrs. Donovan gazed at Dawn with sympathy in her red-veined eyes. "I see."

Dawn stood up. "I should probably get home," she said. "You know."

"Okay." Jane gave her a rather gloomy smile. "Good luck tomorrow."

"Yeah," Jake added. "Good luck, Dawn."

Chapter Eighteen

On Sunday morning, Dawn woke up early, yanked out of a deep sleep when she almost choked on a mouthful of phlegm.

Her heart thumped. It had happened.

She jumped out of bed and rushed to the mirror. To her surprise, the same familiar face looked back at her, a little bleary-eyed but otherwise perfectly normal. No green skin. No clumps of missing hair.

Choking back the drool, she leaned closer, not quite daring to believe her eyes. She hadn't changed.

At least not yet . . .

"Dawn!" Her mother looked up with happy surprise on her face when Dawn rushed into the kitchen. "Happy birthday! You look — the same."

Dawn nodded. "Does it always happen right

away?" she demanded. "Like, could I still change later today?"

Her mother traded a look with her father, who was at the stove frying bacon. "It's been known to happen," Mrs. Romero said. "But this certainly increases the chances that you'll stay as you are."

That didn't sound certain enough for Dawn. She grabbed a slice of toast and slathered it with jam. If she was going to start craving meat any second now, she wanted to enjoy one more normal breakfast while she had the chance. Her parents could eat that bacon.

She opened her mouth to take a bite but had to suck back a tendril of drool first. Yes, she'd better enjoy that toast while she could. . . .

Dawn still hadn't changed by the time Luna stopped in after lunch.

"Happy birthday!" Luna said when she came in.

"Thanks." Dawn was sitting in the kitchen, trying to read a magazine while her father cleaned up the lunch dishes. Normally, that was Dawn's job on weekends, but after she'd almost dropped the same plate twice, he'd insisted on taking over.

Dawn wasn't finding it any easier to focus on her magazine than on the dishes. Every time she had to swallow back another mouthful of saliva, she jumped up and ran to the mirror in the powder room to see if her skin was turning green.

Luna leaned against the counter. She was dressed in her riding clothes. "Doing anything fun to celebrate today?"

"Oh, sure," Dawn muttered, reaching up to run a hand over her thick dark hair. Still all there as far as she could tell. "I'm having a blast."

Luna giggled. "That's what I figured. I'm on my way to the stable. Want to come?" She bent to pat Mr. Marmalade, who had appeared out of nowhere and started twisting in and out around her legs, purring loudly.

Dawn stared at her cat gloomily. At least Mr. Marmalade was totally used to zombies now. He probably wouldn't freak out too much if and when his owner suddenly turned into one.

"I can't go today," she told her cousin. "I mean, what if I started to change while I'm riding?"

"So what if you do?" Luna shrugged as if the thought were the most normal thing in the world.

"The horses won't care. And everyone else there is already a zombie, remember?"

"She has a point, kiddo," Dawn's dad put in with a smile. "Go have fun. It'll take your mind off things."

Dawn opened her mouth to argue. Then she shrugged. Maybe they were right.

"Okay," she said. "Give me a minute to change clothes."

Hours later, Ms. Kazemi poked her head into Skip's stall, where Dawn and Luna were giggling as they braided the patient gelding's mane with multicolored ribbons. The stable owner rolled her eyes when she saw what they were doing.

"Your parents just called looking for you," she told Dawn. "They want you to head home for dinner."

"It's dinnertime already?" Dawn glanced at her wrist before remembering that she'd taken off her watch and put it in her pocket when she bathed Skip after their lesson. The skin of her arm was the same color as always. No green at all.

Both her parents were in the kitchen when she got home. They looked up quickly, then smiled. "Hi, kiddo," Dawn's father said. "How were the ponies today?"

"Fine." Dawn swallowed back a mouthful of saliva. Being at the barn had helped her forget it was her birthday. But her worries had all come rushing back on the bike ride home. "Listen, how long is it going to be before I change into a zombie? Because I can't take this waiting much longer."

Her parents traded a look. "I think it's safe to say you're not going to change," her mother said. "You'd be showing at least some signs by now."

"That's the thing," Dawn said. "I am showing a sign." She told her parents about the drool.

Her mother looked concerned. "And how long has this been going on?"

"I don't know. A few weeks, maybe?" Dawn shrugged. "It started pretty soon after we moved here, I think."

"That's odd," her father said. "I've never heard of drool being the first sign of the change. I thought the hair and skin effects usually came first."

"They do." Dawn's mother stared at Dawn. She had that scientist look in her eyes. "Let me call Dr. Pruitt. I think he'll want to hear about this."

She hurried toward the phone. Dawn looked at her father. "So do you think I'm changing?"

He squeezed her hand. "I don't know, kiddo. Try not to worry."

A short while later, Dawn and her parents walked into the Z Corp lab. Dr. Pruitt was already there. He rushed to greet them.

"Happy birthday, Dawn," he said. "Now, what's this about some drool?"

With her mother's help, Dawn explained her symptoms. Dr. Pruitt nodded thoughtfully and asked her to open her mouth so he could take a look. But as soon as he leaned closer, he let out a loud sneeze.

"Excuse me," he said, sniffling and backing away. "I'm quite sensitive to patchouli."

"Patchouli?" Dawn wondered if that was some strange new zombie symptom she'd never heard of before. "What's that?"

"It's a scent," her mother explained. "It's probably in that perfume we gave you."

"Oh." Dawn had dabbed on a little more perfume when she'd changed out of her riding clothes just now. Doing that had become a habit — like checking her teeth after eating spinach, or brushing her teeth before bed. "Sorry about that," she said as Dr. Pruitt sneezed again.

"It's quite all right," he said, sniffling loudly. "All it takes is a whiff of the stuff to set me off."

Dawn gasped as she realized something. "Wait," she said. "Could I be allergic to patchouli?"

Her father looked confused, but her mother caught on right away. "When did you say your symptoms started?" she asked.

Dawn stopped to think about it. "The first time I really noticed it was on my first day at VCJH," she said. "I put on lots of my perfume that day." She didn't explain why — she was a little embarrassed now, that she'd been so worried about smelling even faintly of zombie.

"I see." Dr. Pruitt stroked his chin, staring at Dawn from a safe distance. "And you've been wearing that same cologne regularly?"

"Every day," Dawn said. "I've used up more than half the bottle."

"There's a sink over there." Her mother pointed. "Go scrub that stuff off yourself and see if your symptoms subside."

Dawn did as she was told, using lots of soap and hot water until she was pretty sure there was no trace of Les Cayes left on her skin. Dr. Pruitt waited until she was finished, then stepped forward.

"May I take a look now?" he asked.

Dawn nodded and opened her mouth, tipping back her head. Dr. Pruitt grabbed a tongue depressor and peered in, poking around here and there. Dawn could feel saliva dripping off her lower lip, but she tried to stay still.

"Well?" her father asked after a few moments.

Dr. Pruitt stepped back. "It's difficult to tell," he said. "There does still seem to be excess saliva production. But if she's allergic to patchouli or another ingredient in that perfume, it could take a while for the effects to wear off."

That wasn't the answer Dawn was hoping for. "So you still don't know if I'm going to turn zombie?" she asked, wiping the drool from her chin.

"Not based on your mouth, no." Dr. Pruitt shrugged. "However, I can tell you it would be highly unusual for excess saliva to be the first symptom."

"But unusual doesn't mean impossible, right?" Dawn glanced at her mother. That was something she said sometimes.

"Right," Mrs. Romero said. "But maybe we can try something else. If you're up for it."

"Anything," Dawn said immediately. "I just want to know."

Dr. Pruitt nodded. "All right. Most people do change immediately on their thirteenth birthday. However, even those who are a little slower will show early signs of changes in their skin. We'll have to take a sample and examine it under the microscope."

"If you're changing, we'll be able to see it," Dawn's mother added.

"Good." Dawn shivered, suddenly more nervous than ever. "What do I need to do?"

"Sit down right here." Dr. Pruitt pulled out a chair. Then he spent about three hours washing his hands. That was how long it seemed to Dawn, anyway. Finally, he pulled out a scalpel and scraped some skin off Dawn's arm. It hurt a little, but she barely noticed.

"How soon can you tell?" she demanded.

Her mother was bustling around nearby, washing her hands and pulling equipment out of cabinets. "Try to be patient, Dawn," she said, sounding distracted. "It's more important to be accurate than to be fast."

Dawn's father put a hand on Dawn's arm. "Come sit down," he said. "It'll go faster if we stay out of the way."

For the next few minutes, Dawn had a hard time sitting still. She watched as her mother and Dr. Pruitt prepared a slide with her skin sample and then huddled over the microscope, taking turns peering into the eyepiece and conferring in soft voices.

Finally, they turned around. Both of them were smiling.

"Good news, Dawn," her mother said. "You're not changing."

"I'm not?" Dawn's heart leaped. "I won't turn into a zombie? Are you sure?"

"Quite," Dr. Pruitt confirmed. "Your skin shows absolutely none of the telltale signs. It seems you're a carrier just like your parents."

Dawn's father reached over and gave her a hug. "You beat the odds, kiddo," he said. "Like you kept telling us, you had a twenty-five percent chance of *not* changing. And that's what happened."

"Wow." Dawn wasn't sure how to feel at first.

Her mother gave her a hug as well. "I guess we didn't have to move to Vespertine after all," she said. "I'm sorry your whole life was uprooted for nothing. We were just afraid of what might happen if —"

"I know," Dawn interrupted. "It's okay."

Her first thought was that now they could go home. She could return to her old life, her old friends, her old home. The normal, outside world.

Was that still what she wanted, though? Moving here had been difficult at first. But there had been good things, too. Lots of them, now that she thought about it. She'd made some amazing friends, like Luna and the twins. Her new stable was great, and her parents were already talking to Ms. Kazemi about letting her lease Skip so she could ride several times a week. Dawn's mother loved living near her family and working at Z Corp. Her father was enjoying his role as a stay-at-home dad and talking about writing that novel he'd never had time for before. Even Mr. Marmalade had adjusted.

And so had Dawn. No, she didn't want to move back home after all. Vespertine *was* her home now.

"It's okay," Dawn said again, hugging her mother back. "I'm glad we moved here."

"Really?" Her mother pulled away, looking shocked.

Dawn laughed. "Really. And I was thinking — it's kind of a pain for Dad to have to drive me all the way to East Valley every day. Besides, the twins will be going to Vespertine Academy now, and Luna's already there. If it's okay with you guys, I was thinking I might give it a try."

Now her mother looked delighted. "Of course!"

"We're so proud of you, kiddo," her father said. "Come on, let's go home. We've kept Dr. Pruitt from his dinner long enough."

They stayed to help Dr. Pruitt clean up the lab. As she carefully stowed the microscope in its cabinet, Dawn looked over the other equipment in there. Who knew — maybe if she decided not to become a vet, she'd end up working as a researcher at Z Corp herself someday.

Dawn finished her dinner quickly and pushed her plate away. "May I be excused?" she asked. "I want to go tell Jake and Jane what happened today."

"Of course." Her mother looked up from her food. "But don't stay too late, all right? You'll have to get up early tomorrow so we can go over and get you signed in at Vespertine Academy."

Dawn felt a shiver of nerves as she hurried next door. How would the twins react when they saw she hadn't changed despite her high percentage?

"Dawn!" Jake looked shocked when he answered the door. "You didn't — uh, I mean happy birthday."

"Thanks. Are you guys in the middle of dinner or anything?" Dawn asked.

"No, we finished a while ago. Come on in." Jake stepped back to let her enter. Then he turned and yelled, "Jane! Dawn's here."

A moment later, Jane appeared. She stopped short in the doorway. "Oh. Seventy-five percent chance, huh?" Her tone was sarcastic and a little resentful.

"I know." For some strange reason, Dawn felt the urge to apologize. "I was surprised, too."

"Well, I guess it's good news for you." Jane wandered into the room and flopped onto the sofa. "You can still go to VCJH and be normal."

"I'm not," Dawn said quickly. "Um, I mean I'm not going to stay at VCJH. I decided to give Vespertine Academy a try."

"Really?" Jake's eyes lit up.

"Uh-huh." Dawn smiled at him. "I mean, all my real friends are going to be there, right?"

Jane still looked wary. "Why?" she demanded. "You don't have to go there. You're not a zombie."

"Yes, I am." For the first time, Dawn realized it was true. She was part of a zombie family. "I have zombie genes, just like you guys. They're just not expressed." She shrugged. "I hope you don't mind being friends with a lowly carrier."

That actually made Jane crack a smile. "Well . . ." she drawled, pretending to mull it over. "I suppose we might be able to get used to hanging out with a carrier. Maybe."

Jake laughed. "Definitely," he corrected. "Don't listen to Jane — she's just a zombie snob."

Jane stuck out her tongue at him, allowing more drool to escape. "Shut up, green-face."

"*You* shut up, droolie." Jake grinned, then glanced at Dawn. "Hey, wait here a sec, okay?"

"Sure." Dawn watched as he hurried out of the room. "Where's he going?" she asked Jane.

Jane smirked. "You'll see."

Jake reappeared seconds later, out of breath and clutching a small box in one hand. "Happy birthday," he blurted out, his cheeks going pink beneath the greenish blotches. "Um, sorry I didn't have a chance to wrap it."

"You got me a present?" Dawn was surprised. She accepted the box and opened it. Inside was a small silver charm.

"It's for your necklace." Jake sounded uncharacteristically shy. "Um, it's a mountain. I got it to represent Vespertine." He shrugged. "I know it doesn't have anything to do with horses, but . . ."

"No, it's great. I love it!" Dawn lifted the charm carefully out of its bed of soft cotton. "I want to add it to my necklace right now."

She unhooked the chain and threaded the new charm on. It nestled right between the large horse charm and the tiny silver boots. "Looks good," Jane said approvingly.

Dawn nodded. Brushing her hair aside, she lifted the necklace back into place, but her fingers fumbled as they tried to work the clasp.

"Here, let me get that." Jake stepped forward.

As he fastened the chain, his hands brushed against Dawn's neck. She shivered a little — but this time, it definitely *wasn't* because she was grossed out. She could smell his zombie scent more clearly than ever without her perfume getting in the way, and feel the cool, slightly slimy touch of his skin.

Why had any of that stuff ever bothered her, any-way? After all, it was just part of who Jake was, and part of all of her new friends and family, too. Part of Dawn's new life — and her new home here in Vespertine.

DON'T MISS ANY OF THE
OTHER ROTTEN APPLE BOOKS!
READ ON FOR THREE
BONE-CHILLING SNEAK
PEEKS, IF YOU DARE . . .

MEAN GHOULS

As if he knew what she was thinking, Sam leaned over and whispered, "Transformation happens very, very slowly. It takes centuries to become a full zombie."

That was supposed to make Megan feel better, but it didn't. "Centuries?" she gasped.

"You're immortal now," Sam told her. "Didn't anyone tell you that?"

She thought back to the things that she knew about zombies. She didn't recall Zach saying that she'd live forever. It wasn't on the websites she'd looked at either.

Megan would be twelve years old from now on. With no real friends at her new school, that didn't sound so good.

ZOMBIE DOG

As she dragged the can the rest of the way to the curb, Becky was thinking so hard that she was barely aware of how much stronger the rotting smell that had hung around all day was getting. When she reached the curb, though, it flooded her senses so much that she had to let go of the can to cough and cover her face with her hands. It was heavy and foul, even worse than it had been the night before.

Suddenly, from the sidewalk beside her came a thick, wet-sounding snarl.

A small animal was moving toward her slowly, its green eyes shining unnaturally in the glow from the streetlights. She realized that it was dragging its left hind leg behind it, moving painfully. Becky froze as the creature moved closer to her, stepping into the light.

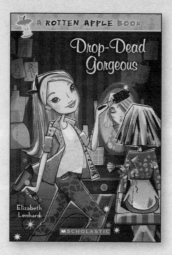

DROP-DEAD GORGEOUS

When the girls arrived at the far corner of the square, they found that the boys had stopped in their tracks!

"Hey, they did wait for us," Rachel said.

But it turned out the boys weren't being polite. They were frozen in place while someone — or something — made its way toward them.

The creature was wrapped from head to toe in gauze bandages. These were the only things that seemed to hold its limbs in place. One arm oozed green blood and dangled down by the monster's knees. Its head was a mass of bandages and black spiderwebs (complete with spiders). Its lips were black and shiny and its teeth — seen through a ghastly smile — were green, yellow, and brown.

The monster was so terrifying, it had to be real!

POISON APPLE BOOKS

The Dead End

This Totally Bites!

Miss Fortune

Now You See Me...

Midnight Howl

Her Evil Twin

Curiosity Killed the Cat

At First Bite

THRILLING.

BONE-CHILLING.

THESE BOOKS

HAVE BITE!

HAUNTINGS

A spine-tingling scare in every sto

READ THEM ALL!

YOU'RE IN FOR THE
FRIGHT OF YOUR LIFE!